Caught Offside

ALSO BY ANDREA MONTALBANO

Out of Bounds

Caught Offside

Andrea Montalbano

sourcebooks
jabberwocky

Published by Sourcebooks Jabberwocky, an imprint of Sourcebooks, Inc.
P.O. Box 4410, Naperville, Illinois 60567-4410
(630) 961-3900
Fax: (630) 961-2168
www.sourcebooks.com

Library of Congress Cataloging-in-Publication Data

Names: Montalbano, Andrea, author.
Title: Caught offside / Andrea Montalbano.
Description: Naperville, Illinois : Sourcebooks Jabberwocky, [2017] | Series: Soccer Sisters ; [2] | Summary: Val feels left out when her soccer teammates focus on boys rather than soccer, and when Jessie tries to push her out she considers leaving the Brookville Breakers.
Identifiers: LCCN 2017002456 |
Subjects: | CYAC: Soccer--Fiction. | Teamwork (Sports)--Fiction. | Friendship--Fiction. | Bullying--Fiction. | Belonging (Social psychology)--Fiction. | Security (Psychology)--Fiction. | Family life--Fiction.
Classification: LCC PZ7.M76342 Cau 2017 | DDC [Fic]--dc23 LC record available at https://lccn.loc.gov/2017002456

Source of Production: Versa Press, East Peoria, Illinois, USA
Date of Production: August 2017
Run Number: 5010103

Printed and bound in the United States of America.
VP 10 9 8 7 6 5 4 3 2 1

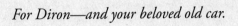

For Diron—and your beloved old car.

1

Are we late again?" a voice asked from the backseat. It was Val Flores's BFF—her teammate, her sister from another mother, number eight on the Brookville Breakers, center midfielder, sometimes-difficult-but-overall-fan-favorite—Makena Walsh, a.k.a. Mac. Val looked at the car clock and then turned to answer.

"Believe it or not, only like two minutes," she said. "Might be a record!"

Makena gave a small cheer, gathered up her ball and water bottle, and zipped up her jacket. Val loved that her buddy was born ready for action.

"It's freezing," Makena said, exhaling a puff of air. Even in the small car, the temperature was chilly. Val and Makena lived in neighboring suburbs just north of New York City. It was midwinter, and the world seemed like a giant ice block since the start of the year.

"You know it's not much warmer inside the Doom," Val said, nodding toward the enormous white indoor soccer facility where all the teams practiced. Its real name was the Dome, but the girls found it creepy and cold.

The girls shivered in unison. The only winter soccer facility near Brookville was nothing more than a turf field covered by a giant inflated tent. It looked like half of a massive, grimy golf ball sticking out of the ground. Inside there was no heat except the kind made by all the teams running, kicking, and practicing on the three fields.

"Papi, just let us out here, *por favor*," Val said sweetly to her father, Miguel, in her regular mix of English and Spanish.

"*Sí, pero, m'ija*, where are your sweatpants?" Miguel asked with an accent. He motioned toward Val's outfit. She was wearing only a sweatshirt, jacket, and soccer shorts, and her legs were bare at the knees. Nubby goose bumps covered the entire middle section of Val's legs.

"Oh, I forgot them. It's fine, Papi, we'll be running the whole time," Val answered quickly.

Miguel's face registered concern. The wind howled, shaking the car slightly. Val thought the weather was conspiring with her father.

"Look," Val said. "I'll just pull my socks up over my knees and pull my shorts down low, and there will be only a tiny bit of skin showing." Val yanked at her white tube socks, stretching the nylon fabric up over her knee.

"See?" she said to her father, trying to get the furrow of worry from his brow to release. Miguel seemed to relax momentarily, until a ripping sound filled the tiny car.

"*¡Aye!*" Miguel yelled.

"Ugh," Val muttered to herself. Looking down, she could feel and see the giant hole she'd torn in her tube sock.

"What the heck was that?" Makena asked, leaning forward.

"I totally trashed my sock." Val held up her leg to show the damage. A tear, about six inches across, exposed the back of her right calf. Val looked at the threadbare fabric. Man, those socks were really old. Makena started to laugh, and Miguel rolled his eyes.

"Do you have another sock?" Makena asked.

Val shook her head. "Who carries three socks around?"

"Another pair of socks!" Makena yelled with a laugh.

Val looked at the clock again. She had to think fast. Searching her soccer bag, she found nothing but a half-eaten snack bar and an empty water bottle.

"*Mi amor*, you cannot go to practice like that," Miguel said firmly.

"Oh, man, we are so late now. Coach Lily is going to make us do, like, a million push-ups," Makena said. She looked at Val's leg. "What are you going to do? Your sock is hanging on…uh…literally by a thread."

Val expanded her search to her father's car. She fumbled under her seat and pulled out a pile of papers and an old pair of shorts.

"Papi, this is why it's so cold in the car! Look!" Val showed her father the crack in the floor of the old sedan. Icy air was flowing in.

"*¿Dónde?*" Miguel asked.

"*Aquí*, look," Val said. *The car is old and in bad shape*, Val thought. Just another something new they couldn't afford. She shrugged and watched as Miguel felt under the seat. His eyes opened wide when he felt the cold air hit his fingers. As if on cue, another gust of wind whipped through the little car.

"Oh, look! This is perfect!" Val exclaimed, emerging from under the passenger's seat with a small piece of camouflage fabric that looked like something from the U.S. Army.

"What is that?" Makena asked.

"It's a bandanna," Val said. "Watch this." She took

the camouflaged square, folded it into a triangle, and then folded it again into a long strip. Quickly, she wrapped the bandanna over the hole in her sock, folded the torn sock over the top, and tucked the ends inside. The result was a white sock with a trendy camouflage trim.

"OK, I don't know how you did that," Makena said, her head tilted slightly, "but that's actually pretty cool!"

"And it better keep you warm," Miguel added.

"Let's go!" Val exclaimed, and the two giggling girls scrambled out of the car. A jumble of bags, balls, and jackets rolled into the dark, icy parking lot.

"I'll see you two *locas* later," Miguel said with a chuckle.

"Yes, Chloe's driving us home, and, remember, she's staying for dinner," Val reminded her father excitedly. The trio—Mac, Val, and Chloe—had started a new after-practice dinner tradition: dinner at Rosa's, the gourmet shop and restaurant owned by Makena's father. It was in Brookville, where Makena and most of the Breakers lived. For as long as Val could remember, her dad had been the manager.

Miguel nodded and waved as he pulled away. The two girls hurried toward the entrance, holding on to each other tightly as their flat indoor shoes provided no traction on the super-dangerous patches of black ice.

"Hey, wait up!" they heard a voice cry. It was their teammate Jessie. She trudged up behind Makena and Val.

"Hey, Jessie," Val said, slowing down to wait for her teammate. Jessie was one of the tallest girls on the team and a really strong defender. She had brown hair and dark eyebrows.

"That parking lot is a mess. My mom had to drop me way back there," Jessie said, gesturing behind her. Turning her head, she noticed Miguel's car. "Jeez, Val, nice ride. What a clunker."

"I know," Val said, laughing. "But my father loves that old wreck for some reason."

"Let's gooo already!" Makena chided.

The three girls pushed their way through the revolving door and into the soccer dome.

Val shivered when she got inside. "It's just as cold in here!"

"Well, at least there isn't any wind," Makena said, and all three girls looked up to the Dome's ceiling just as an icy gust made the lights sway in unison.

"Yikes, I hope this place doesn't fall in on us," Jessie said.

"It's fine," Val said, scanning the fields. "Where's our team?"

"There they are." Makena pointed and ran.

Val spied the Breakers gathered on the far side and knew immediately that the three of them had missed warm-up completely. The rest of the team was gathered around their coach, Lily James, who was already in the middle of explaining the first drill. Jasmine, Harper, and Ariana all had annoyed looks on their faces.

"Uh-oh," Val whispered when she caught up to Makena. "I'm sorry to make you so late again."

Mac just smiled and shrugged.

"Val, what's that on your leg?" Jessie asked as the girls jogged over to meet their team.

"Oh, nothing," Val answered as she and Makena shared a smile.

"Nice of you girls to join us," Lily said, holding up her hand to stop them from coming any closer. "That's two full laps and twenty push-ups. All three of you. Get going. Practice is at six o'clock, not six-oh-eight."

Val, Makena, and Jessie sighed together and then turned away from the group of girls and started their run around the field.

"Sorry," Val said again.

"Oh, forget about it already. It's no biggie!" Mac said. "Let's go. At least we can get warm!"

"Oh, man, I hate running laps, and I hate push-ups

more," Jessie complained as soon as they rounded the first corner. "My father couldn't find his stupid keys. It's not my fault I was late."

"Well, it doesn't bother me," Makena said. "I just don't want to miss too many of the drills." She picked up the pace. "Let's go!"

Val smiled at her soccer-obsessed best friend. There was nothing about soccer that Makena didn't love. And there was pretty much nothing about Makena that Val didn't love. They were just a perfect pair. Physically, the two girls could not have looked more different. Makena was tall, and Val was tiny. Makena was fair with Irish freckles and bright eyes that were a mix of green, blue, and yellow. Val was from Mexico. Her skin was darker, like her eyes and hair. The two girls had been friends since they were babies. Makena's mom used to say they were "buddies in buckets," buckets being the baby car seats with a handle that looked, well, like buckets. Val and Makena had learned to love soccer together, playing behind Rosa's from the time they could walk. The busboys and servers, most of them Hispanic, adored the little girls who loved *fútbol*. Val and Makena were never without teammates. Anyone on break was ready to play with the two tiny and adorable soccer nuts.

Val kept pace with Makena and Jessie but jogged just a few steps behind them, warming up slowly. She could hear the howl of the wind outside and feel the cold rush from the ventilation cracks in the Dome's lining. Val was drawn to the line of lights hanging from the ceiling. She noticed that each light was contained in a metal cage so that when (not if) it got hit with a ball, no glass shattered down on the players. *Who thought of that?* Val wondered.

"Look at the lights," Val said, intrigued.

Makena looked up. "It's like a creepy, cold disco in here tonight."

"Speaking of disco," Jessie said. "Mac, do you know who you're going to ask to the dance?"

"No clue," Makena answered while rounding the last corner. "Haven't thought about it and still trying to get out of it."

"Dance?" Val had no idea what they were talking about.

"Oh, this dumb school thing, the Snow Fairy Dance," Makena said. "It raises money for charity, so my mom is making me go."

"Making you go? I am sooo excited," Jessie said. "This dance is the event of the year. And the best part is that the girls get to ask the boys and the boys have to say yes to the first girl who invites them."

"Best part?" Makena asked. "Try nightmare. All the girls are freaking out about which boy to invite. It's bad enough to have to be asked. It's worse to have to be the *asker*."

"What do you mean, the boy has to say yes? Boys can't ask girls to the dance?" Val was confused.

"Well," said Jessie. "I guess, technically, but the tradition is that the girls ask the boys, and the boys say yes because, if the boy says no, then he can't say yes to anyone else, and so, basically, he can't go."

Val rolled her eyes. "This all sounds really *dumb*."

Jessie frowned and kept talking. "It's not dumb at all! It is super fun, and when you get there, it's just a giant party and everyone's there."

It didn't sound great to Val. She had yet to find her first crush and was glad she went to a different school and all this dance nonsense was going on at Brookville.

"Well, I already know who I'm asking," Jessie boasted. "And I've got to do it right away because he's so popular, I know he'll be picked right up."

"Who?" Val asked, mildly curious.

"Oh, right. Like I'm going to tell *you*!" Jessie said.

Val was taken aback by Jessie's sharp response. "Whatever," she replied defensively. "I don't even live in Brookville or go to your school."

Val attended middle school in Highland Ferry. Miguel, and lots of other folks who lived in Highland Ferry, worked for people in Brookville. Brookville was mostly large homes, restaurants, and pricey boutiques. Val's middle school didn't offer a soccer team for girls nor did her town, which was why she started playing on the Brookville squad. That, and she and Makena were inseparable.

Val sprinted ahead of Jessie for the final leg of the warm-up run and plopped down close to the rest of the team to stretch. There were only nine girls at practice because the winter season was optional and the team was smaller. They played games with seven players on each side instead of eleven. The fields were also smaller, but the tighter spaces suited Val's game perfectly. She was a striker and had a reputation for her amazing speed and dribbling abilities. Even though she was smaller than most of the rest of the team and twelve, young for her grade, that didn't matter at all in indoor soccer. It was skill and quick think-ing that made Val stand out even more than she did during outdoor season.

Val started on her push-ups as Makena and Jessie caught up. Val watched Jessie finish her last lap with Makena and thought Jessie was acting weird about this dance. Val was much more interested in soccer.

"All the way down, girls!" a voice teased. Val looked up from her second push-up to see Chloe Gordon, hands on hips, standing over her. Chloe smiled at Val and offered her hand when Val was finally done with her last late-for-practice push-up.

"I'm so glad you're here," Chloe said. "All these girls have gone completely nuts."

"Because we're late?" Val asked, worried that her teammates were angry with her.

Chloe laughed. "No, because of this dumb dance. It's nonstop negotiation. I can't understand why they're so worked up. It's annoying."

"Oh, no. More dance drama? Jessie already freaked out on me about it." Val glanced at the rest of her teammates, who were deep in conversation, hardly paying attention to the passing drill Coach Lily had set up for them. Chloe rolled her eyes, and Val smiled. She knew her friend would never let anything social concern her. Chloe Gordon was by far the most popular girl at her school. For starters, she was gorgeous. She had the straightest, longest, most perfect platinum hair. Her locks could inspire Taylor Swift to write a chart-topping revenge song. She'd been a ballet dancer since she was three and had so far sashayed her way around the whole awkward tween phase.

The Gordons also lived in the biggest and fanciest house in Brookville, and the family even had a driver to shuttle the kids around. Val was one of the few people who knew Chloe's life wasn't perfect, but when it came to something like a dance, her buddy had it covered.

"Hey, Chloe!" Jessie said, arriving with Makena. They started their push-ups.

Chloe laughed at her friends. "How was the nice jog?"

Makena smiled. "Well, I'm not freezing anymore!"

"OK, Lily told me to tell you the drill," Chloe said.

Val could see Lily setting up cones on the far side of the field.

"We're doing three versus two. You, me, and Val are starting on offense. Jessie, you're on defense, over there with Jasmine."

"I love three-v-two's!" Val said. Three offensive players started at midfield and tried to score on two defenders and Ariana in goal. Because they outnumbered the defenders by one player, the offense was expected to get a shot off every single time. The key, Val knew, was that very first pass.

Lily blew her whistle, and Val started off with the ball on the right side. Chloe was on the left, and Makena was in her spot in the middle. Val quickly tapped the ball with her left foot and dribbled sharply at Jasmine, the defender on her side. The trick was to draw Jasmine to her by moving toward the goal quickly. The defender had no choice but to try to take the ball, or Val would be in a position to just go straight to the goal and shoot.

Jasmine approached, crouching low, and then back-pedaled, shadowing Val like Spider-Man as she pushed toward the goal. She watched Val's feet carefully, looking for an opening to steal the ball but also trying to slow her down and herd her to the outside of the field. Some players made the mistake of stabbing at the ball with their foot, getting off balance and making it easy for an offender like Val to slip past and get a cross off to the middle of the field. But Jasmine was an experienced defender; she didn't rush.

Val dribbled, keeping her eyes up and ears open.

"Through ball!" she heard a voice yell and saw that Makena was making her move—a diagonal run toward the goal. Jessie was slow to respond, and Makena broke free. Val passed the ball on the outside of Jasmine, and Makena collected it easily. Then Val made her run. In soccer, you have to pass and move. You never just observe the action. Ball watching was a sin on the Breakers. Makena crossed the ball to Chloe, who was wide open in front of the net. Chloe laid it off to Val, who was flying in and fired off a screamer.

The goalie, Ariana, had no chance as the ball slammed into the back of the net.

Val, Makena, and Chloe high-fived in the middle of the field and then jogged back to half-field.

"Stop!" Coach Lily halted the drill. The girls slowed. "Everyone freeze. Val, Mac, and Chloe, get back into the original formation. Jessie and Jasmine, you too."

The girls shared a look. This wasn't good. Lily grabbed the ball and passed it back to Val.

"OK, Val, now at half-speed, dribble down the line again." Val sprinted back into place and did as she was told, repeating the same path but much more slowly.

Lily continued, "OK, now, Jasmine, you did a good job of slowing Val down. Makena, you made an excellent run to the line. Jessie? Where did you make your mistake?"

Jessie shrugged her shoulders and looked at the ground, mumbling, "Dunno."

"You let Makena get ball-side of you, and instead of following her on her run, you were just watching and not really covering anybody."

Jessie's shoulders sagged, and she looked at the ground.

"OK, now, Mac, make that run again," Lily said, guiding Jessie gently by the arm. "Jessie, now, you stay with her, always keeping yourself between the goal and the player, in this case, Mac. Try it again, girls, but this time, Chloe, you start with the ball."

The next few runs went much more smoothly, and before Val knew it, Lily called for a water break. As Val jogged over to the sidelines, she felt a rush of cold air hit her calf.

"Here." Chloe ran up to Val and handed her the camouflage bandanna.

"Oh, thanks," Val said, grateful to be able to cover up. "I'm getting goose bumps already!"

"Hey, Val, you can't afford a whole sock?" Jessie said in a joking voice.

Val picked up the bandanna and retied it over the hole in her sock. "I guess I better get some new ones."

"Seriously. And while you're at it, a new ride." Jessie was laughing as she said this, but Val heard an edge in her voice.

"Well, I think the bandanna is pretty cool," Chloe said. "Maybe I'll wear one next practice."

Val flashed Chloe a smile of gratitude and again felt surprised at Jessie. She began to wonder if maybe Jessie was mad at her. Val tried to recall anything she might have said or done to anger her teammate. Val had scored every time she got the ball during the last drill, but that was pretty normal. Val was about to ask her if everything was all right when a huge gust of wind blew open a set of doors at the entrance. A blast of icy air rushed onto the field, and the girls shrieked their disapproval and fear. One of the coaches rushed to secure the flapping door. The Dome took on an eerie feel as everyone stopped playing. It was oddly quiet except for the howling wind. The kids on the fields looked up as the lights swayed precariously over their heads.

Immediately, whistles blew as coaches gathered their teams.

"Breakers! Over here!" Lily called. "Get out from under that light!"

The glass might not break, but all the lights looked to Val like they might come crashing down. Two other coaches continued to struggle with the door. Every time it seemed they had secured the revolving panes, another arctic blast would rip through, making a terrible crashing noise as one door slammed against the other. No one could come in or go out the main entrance. The swinging lights cast crazy shadows on the sides of the Dome, and the temperature started to plummet. Val and the rest of the Breakers huddled together, wondering what was coming next. It wasn't long before the power flickered off and on and then off again, leaving the Dome totally, utterly dark.

"I don't like this," Mac said, shivering.

The lights came back on quickly, but the door continued to slam, and then the entire dome itself seemed to be heaving with the violent winter squalls.

"OK, I really don't like this," Mac repeated, grabbing Val by the arm.

"Girls, let's start moving toward that emergency exit," Lily said, pointing to a door across the field. "Stay together."

"Just get your jackets if they're close and follow me. Everyone hold hands," Lily instructed. All the girls grabbed hands and arms. Lily latched on to Val's arm to lead them and said, "Stick close."

"I dropped my ball!" Jasmine cried. Her pink-and-neon-orange soccer ball rolled across the turf.

"Leave it," Lily ordered. Val felt Lily's grip tighten.

The Breakers moved like a shuffling train, arms linked, toward the exit. Val had Lily on one side and Makena on the other. Makena was squeezing Val's upper arm like a vise. Another howl of the wind seemed to shift the entire ceiling, and for the first time, Val was a little frightened too. The Breakers picked up the pace to a trot, the neon-red exit sign beckoning their escape.

When they had just twenty feet to go, the power cut out for good. Val and the rest of the team were engulfed by blackness. Only the exit sign shone dimly ahead. Val looked up, but the top of the Dome was as black as the ground in front of her.

"I don't like this at all," she said.

2

OK, girls, we're going to keep moving toward that sign and gather outside. It's going to be really cold. Try to get your coats on and stick together as soon as we get out."

"If we get out…" Ariana said in a nervous voice.

"Of course we're getting out," Val said calmly. "The door is right there."

The team shuffled forward, arms entwined. Lily found the door handle with an outstretched arm and let go of Val. Val could hear Lily grunting to try to open the door against the howling wind.

"Val, Mac, help me," Lily commanded.

The two girls moved forward and used the weight of their bodies to shove the door with their shoulders. Val was nearly a head shorter and nine months younger, and she had always been small for her age. Still, she was tough, wiry, and strong. Mostly, she was determined. She had grit.

"On three," Lily said. "One…two…three!"

Val leaned against the door and pushed with all her might. She used her legs. She grunted. Finally, the door cracked slightly, and a blast of wind hit her right in the face. It startled her, and she tried to catch her breath. The door slammed back shut.

"Again," Lily said. "Girls, help us."

"We can do it!" Val yelled. "Come on!"

More of the Breakers gathered behind Lily, Val, and Makena, and they all pushed together. Suddenly, the wind caught the metal door and slammed it all the way open with an alarming and violent crash. The team jumped and screamed.

Val wanted to get out of the Dome, but outside wasn't much better. The wind was whipping past with a creepy howl. The immediate area behind the Dome was pitch-black too. The only light was from a building in the distance.

"Whoa. The whole area must have lost power," Chloe said from behind Val.

"OK, let's go. Everyone out," Lily said. "I know it's cold, but we can't stay in here. It's too dangerous. If you have a jacket, get it on. Keep your fingers in your pockets, and we'll head toward the parking lot and get into the cars."

Val and the Breakers shuffled into the cold blackness.

"Maybe living in California would be nice," Makena joked.

"Or Florida," Jasmine chimed in with a shiver. "I never thought I'd say this, but I'd be happy to move in with my grandparents."

"Or Hawaii!" added Ariana. "We can start a surf team! Called the Bubblers."

"Anywhere but this frozen Popsicle stand!" Makena yelled.

Val loved that her teammates could kid around at a time like this. As a group, they had been through muddy losses and sunny wins, and Val knew that adversity always brought them closer together. Plus, they were a giggly crew.

Lily shuttled the girls forward, counting heads as they exited the doomed dome. Soon, they were stumbling on rocks and roots in the wooded area that led back to the parking lot. Like a welcoming North Star, a small beam of light illuminated the path ahead. Val looked behind her to see where the light was coming from. Chloe was holding up her cell phone.

She shrugged and smiled. "Flashlight app. Never leave home without it."

Arms linked, the girls moved en masse to the parking lot in front of the Dome. A group of frightened parents had gathered at the main entrance, unable to get inside because the entrance door was still unsecured. They rushed forward to gather their kids. Jasmine's mother and Jessie's father were the first Breaker parents to reach the team.

"Are you girls all right?" Mrs. Manikas asked the team. "The whole far side of the Dome looks like it's about to collapse!"

"I can take some of you home," Lily offered. "I have my phone and can send out a team text." Most of the parents had just dropped the girls off. It would be a few minutes before they came back to pick them up. Val wondered how she, Mac, and Chloe would get to the restaurant. She rubbed her icy knees in the cold and pulled her jacket tighter, suddenly wishing she had listened to her father and worn sweatpants after all.

"Chloe, do you want a ride home with me?" Jessie asked.

"Oh, thanks, but Karl is coming to drive me. I just texted him," Chloe replied casually. "Mac and Val are coming with me, Coach."

"OK, girls, I'll be in touch about this weekend," Lily

said, watching as one by one the girls' parents arrived to get them out of the cold. "Game is home this weekend, so I'll have to work on getting us a new location, or we'll have no choice but to forfeit."

The Breakers shrieked in horror. Forfeiting was not in their vocabulary. There were only two games left in the indoor season, and they were heading for a showdown for their first-ever indoor title. A forfeit would throw that all away. Val sneered at the sky. She was sick of winter.

"I'll find a field," Lily said, trying to reassure them.

"Chloe, are you sure you don't need a ride?" Jessie asked again. "We can take you home if you don't want to wait. It's really cold out here."

"Yeah, I'm sure, but thanks. Karl will be here soon." Karl, Val knew, was the man who drove Chloe around when her parents couldn't. The first time Val heard that Chloe's family had a driver, she thought she was living in some kind of Disney movie. No one in Val's world had anything like that. But Chloe's mom and dad both worked constantly, and Chloe and her brother had many after-school activities, so they hired Karl to drive the two kids wherever they needed to go.

"Are you sure? It's really cold out here," Jessie asked one more time.

Chloe looked surprised that Jessie wouldn't let it go.

"I'm good," Chloe said firmly.

Even in the darkness, Val saw a look of consternation flash over Jessie's face. Val smiled at Jessie, trying to ease the awkwardness in the air. Instead of returning the smile, Jessie's scowl deepened, and she picked up her bag.

Then she turned on her heel and stormed off without another word.

I didn't fhtink fhis was a Methican resthruant!" Chloe
said, or tried to, as spicy green tomatillo salsa dribbled
down her chin.

Val and Makena stared slack-jawed at their dainty
friend as she shoveled another bite of shrimp taco into
her already-stuffed mouth. Chloe closed her eyes as if
their dinner were transporting her to a happy place. Head
back, chewing, and smiling all at once, she was completely
unaware that her face was a total mess and her cheeks were
stuffed like a gorging hamster's.

If only Taylor Swift could see her now.

Val tried not to laugh but had never imagined such
a sight. She and Makena were used to their fathers' amazing meals, but apparently Chloe and good food were just
getting to know one another. Val was still amazed that she

and Chloe had become such good friends. When Chloe first joined the team, they were U10s, and Makena said Chloe had a reputation for being stuck up and snobby. But over the years, Val and Makena had learned that Chloe was supercool and that, while at school she was popular and seemed to have everything, things at home were a little harder. Chloe's parents really didn't like her playing soccer, and Val had seen Chloe fight with her parents just to stay on the team.

"That. Is. So. Beyond. Amazthing," Chloe announced, finally taking a break. "What's in there?"

"I'm pretty sure it's shrimp, avocados, salsa, a little queso fresco, and a squeeze of lime," Val said with a casual shrug.

"OK, that's crazy delicious," said Chloe, finally having swallowed. "Maybe the best thing I've ever eaten in my life."

"I'm glad you like it!" Makena said. "Tell my dad. Maybe he'll finally listen to us and let Miguel make tacos for the store."

Val nodded. "We've been bugging him for a while. They are so amazing"

"Can we have that again next week?" Chloe asked.

Makena made a face. "If there's practice next week. That was scary tonight."

Val heard a noise and noticed the kitchen door inch open.

"*¿Cómo están mis* superstars?" Miguel asked, poking his head out from the kitchen to check on the girls. The door opened, and Makena's father, Rory, followed right behind.

"Oh, so happy, happy, happy," Chloe answered immediately, patting her belly.

"Wait!" Chloe thought for a moment and then said proudly, "*Muy contenta.*"

Miguel beamed. Chloe and Miguel had made a deal. He would speak more English if she would practice more Spanish. Miguel knew how to speak English but just felt more comfortable in Spanish. Chloe knew only a little Spanish from having studied ballet in Spain the previous summer.

"And full?" Makena's dad asked.

The girls nodded. Val started to ask her father to make the tacos again next week, but Chloe beat her to it.

"Mr. Flores? That was the most amazing thing I have ever eaten in my entire existence on this planet. Even better than the lasagna we had last week. Can you please make it for us again? I can't wait! There was no way I could say all that in Spanish."

"*¡Por supuesto!* Of course!" Miguel answered, and Val thought she saw her father stand a little taller. No one missed the smug glance he shot Makena's dad. Makena and Val cracked up. Both girls enjoyed their fathers' constant sparring over recipes and who could make the most popular dish of the week.

"*Muchas gracias*," Chloe said.

Mr. Walsh stroked the top of Makena's head. "Your mom called. Lily texted all the parents about the Dome collapsing."

"Oh, no, she didn't!" Makena cried. Val and Chloe looked at one another.

"Wait, what?" Val asked. "Back up. It *collapsed*? As in fell down? It was standing when we left."

Miguel put his hand to his mouth. Makena said what they were all thinking. "This is not good."

Makena's mother, Stacey, was a well-established worrier. She was legendary for letting her imagination run wild, anticipating the worst possible outcome and, as a result, occasionally shutting down events that scared her. If Makena's mom thought the Dome had collapsed anywhere near her child, there was a good chance she'd ban winter soccer altogether.

"Yep. The Dome did in fact partially collapse," Makena's dad said. "And yes, Makena, your mother has been informed. Luckily no one was inside, and no one got hurt. It should be fixed and back up in a month or so."

Val thought for a second. "A month!"

"Well, it will at least give me time to calm down my mom," Makena said, and Chloe laughed.

But Val felt a minor shot of panic course through her body. For her, being a part of the Breakers was more than just playing soccer. It made her whole life better. It made her life complete. Even these after-practice dinners meant so much to Val. Since her father was the manager of Rosa's, she spent a lot of nights alone with the television or in the back office of the restaurant. There were only two in her family. Val's mother had died when she was just a baby, and she didn't have any brothers or sisters. Most of her extended family lived in Mexico, Texas, or Michigan, so she saw them only on holidays or in the summer. Val had friends at school, but she couldn't even imagine how empty her life would be without her special team.

Val asked a series of rapid-fire questions. "Where are we going to play? When are we going to get a field? What's going to happen?"

"I have no idea," Makena's dad told the girls. "Lily said she hasn't found a place for you yet."

"Well, what about the game this weekend?" Val asked. "Will we have to forfeit?"

"She's working on it. Take it easy, girls," Makena's dad said gently, and he and Miguel retreated to the kitchen.

Val, Makena, and Chloe tried to get going on their homework, but they were too distracted to get much done. After a few minutes, Makena stretched and yawned. "So, Chloe, who are you inviting to this dance?"

Chloe shrugged. "Oh, I don't know," she said nonchalantly. "Maybe that cute guy Jack from science class." The halfhearted way Chloe delivered this idea made Val happy.

Makena's mouth hung open. "Chloe, Jack is like the best-looking, most athletic, and most popular kid in the school! Him and your brother, I guess."

Chloe remained unimpressed. "Well, I'm definitely not asking my brother. And maybe I won't ask Jack. I think I'd rather he ask me."

"What do you mean?" Val asked. "Jessie told me the girls have to ask the boys and the boys have to say yes."

"Jessie has a lot to learn," Chloe said with a sly smile. "There are ways around this stuff. I might ask Jack if I feel like it. But my brother gave me the scoop."

"Do tell!" Makena said.

Chloe lowered her voice and looked around, as if a horde of seventh and eighth graders were hiding behind the furniture. Chloe's brother, Andrew, was one year older and in eighth grade. "Lots of guys make it clear they don't want to be asked because if they aren't asked, then later they can invite whomever they want."

Val was totally confused. "How can they control if a girl asks them or not? I don't get it. This whole thing is stupid and complicated. I wish it would just go away. Am I the only one worried that the Breakers are about to forfeit their first game ever?"

"If you're annoyed by the dance chat now, just wait," Chloe said.

"Well, Mac, maybe you should invite Brendon," Val said with a snort. She knew mentioning a boy in town who Makena could not stand would get a good reaction.

As if on cue, Makena made a noise that sounded like a cross between a snorting pig and a horse blowing a fly off its lips. Then she pretended she was throwing up. She put her hands to her neck as if she were choking and threw herself on the ground. Val laughed so hard she momentarily forgot her soccer woes. Brendon had stolen Mac's lunchbox and thrown it in the garbage can in second grade, and Mac had held a grudge ever since.

"Actually," Chloe said, "I think Jessie likes Brendon."

"You have got to be kidding me," Makena said, getting up from the floor. "He is one hundred percent unlikable."

Chloe shrugged and said, "Some girls think he's cute."

Makena pretended she was gagging again. Val was starting to think maybe Makena thought he was cute too.

Val considered that day's practice and Jessie's behavior. "Speaking of Jessie, did you guys notice she was being a little weird today?"

"I didn't really notice anything," Makena said, averting her eyes and turning quickly back to her social studies report.

"Nope," Chloe said flatly.

An odd pit of doubt swirled in Val's stomach. She was certain something was bothering Jessie, certain that she had been acting sort of weird and, if Val were honest with herself, mean. But if no one else noticed it, maybe she was imagining it. Val sighed audibly, and Makena looked up from her homework.

"You OK?" Makena asked.

Val started to say what was bothering her but stopped when her dad burst through the door armed with a tray with three flans, all topped with whipped cream.

Chloe actually clapped with joy and made a crazy squeaking noise that brought to Val's mind some kind of bird language. Val herself put up her hand to stop her father from setting a serving of flan in front of her. She'd lost her appetite. Something wasn't right. It wasn't just the Dome of Doom or the dance or even Jessie. Images from the past summer flashed through her mind. Makena and Jessie had gotten into a lot of trouble sneaking out of their hotel room with a guest player named Skylar. They'd both been grounded and nearly suspended from the team, which was really scary for Val. Her team was everything. They had even come up with a team code to help guide them. Val prayed that the drama from the summer was gone for good but had a sinking feeling Jessie might be at it again.

"¿*M'ija?*" Miguel asked again.

"No, *gracias*, Papi, I'm just not hungry."

Perhaps the only thing Val loved as much as playing soccer with her team was watching soccer with her father on Saturday mornings. Today the two were relaxing on the love seat in the living room of their apartment while English Premier League soccer blared from the small television. Earlier that week, Val had invited Makena over to watch the match, but Makena said she couldn't come because she had to do some chores around the house.

She's missing a great game, Val thought, sighing contentedly as her father massaged her foot. She closed her eyes for just a second but then felt an extra-hard squeeze right in the bottom of her instep.

"Ouch!" Val cried as she wrestled her foot away from her agitated father.

Miguel dropped her foot and stood. "*¡Es una falta!*" he shouted at the television.

Val watched the slow-motion replay and, sure enough, saw her favorite player brought down by a wicked tackle just outside the eighteen-yard penalty box. "That was totally a foul!" Val cried, jumping to her feet beside her father. "How could they not call that?"

Play on the pitch continued, even as Zarco lay on the ground, rubbing his ankle, his face grimacing in agony. Val checked how much time was left in the game: just five minutes. The score read Manchester United 2, Manchester City 2. Tied. Manchester United needed to win this game to stay in the top four. A tie was worth only one point in the standings, but a win was worth three.

"Please get up, Zarco…" Val muttered. Javier "Zarco" Merino was her favorite professional player in the whole world, and she knew he was the one guy who could get Manchester United back in the game.

Miguel lowered himself back onto the love seat and said, "*No te preocupes, él es muy fuerte.*"

"I know he's strong, Papi, but he's also still on the ground." Val inched closer to the television, as if Javier could feel her presence. He was writhing in pain now. Val could see his nickname, "Zarco," embroidered on the back of his jersey. Zarco's father and grandfather had both been soccer stars in Mexico, and they all had the same sparkling-blue eyes. Miguel had explained to Val that the name *Zarco* meant blue like a sparkling stream. Like many professional players from Latin America, he went by just one name. A Manchester United teammate finally kicked the ball out of bounds to give Zarco a chance to get back on his feet. Val was relieved to see him start to get up but didn't like the fact that the clock kept ticking.

Val sat back down next to her father, who rubbed her shoulders this time. Val smiled at him. Saturday mornings had always been their special time, but in the past few years, the games had become even more exciting because a Mexican player was finally being seen as a European super-star. Miguel got up from the couch and went to the other room in their small apartment.

"Papi, the game's back on!" Val could hear him rummaging in a plastic bag. He walked back into the room and tossed a dense packet at Val. It bounced on the floor and settled at her feet. Val picked it up and knew what it was immediately. New practice socks.

"*Gracias*, Papi," Val said with a smile, turning back to the game and tearing open the plastic bag filled with two pairs of white soccer socks. Val glanced at the clock and felt another jolt of excitement. Chloe would be there any minute. In the nick of time, their coach had found a field for today's game, and the Breakers had avoided a forfeit. They were playing at another indoor turf facility in a neighboring town until the Dome was fixed.

Val pulled out a pristine pair of new socks and rubbed her fingers across the soft cotton foot. Her father had remembered to get the extra-soft kind. She glanced at her dad as he watched the game. But soon enough, action on the field re-grabbed her attention. Man U was on a flying counterattack in the game's waning seconds. Armen Mardirossian, the other star attacker, had the ball in the corner. He pulled it back with his left and lifted a right-footed cross into the box. Zarco was there, but Val could tell he was at an impossible angle. Even if he could control the ball, he couldn't shoot. Zarco had his back to the goal, and the opposing team's defenders surrounded him, pecking at him like angry chickens. Zarco brought the ball down and guarded it with his body. He looked for an opportunity to shoot. Val stole a glance at the clock. The game was in injury time already. Thirty seconds to score or Manchester United would have to settle for one of its first ties of the season to its nemesis and rival, Manchester City.

"Do something!" Val yelled at the television.

As if he could hear her in cold, rainy England, Zarco made his move. He faked to his right and then turned to his left. Instead of going for the impossible shot, he flicked the ball away from the goal with the outside of his left foot. The ball rolled slowly until a blur in red barreled his way into the box. The blur was Mardirossian. He crunched a left-footed shot, and the ball rocketed toward the goal and slammed into the back of the net.

"Goooooal!" Miguel and Val shouted together as Zarco and Mardirossian celebrated yet another amazing, jaw-dropping, come-from-behind victory.

There was a pounding on the door. "Val!"

Val ran to the door and opened it quickly.

"What the heck is going on in here?" Chloe asked with a laugh. "Did I miss our game or something?"

In their celebration, Miguel and Val hadn't heard her knocking.

"Man U just scored in injury time!" Val told Chloe, grabbing her bag and ball. "Bye, Papi!"

"¡*Tus tacos!*" Miguel yelled after her. *Tacos* was slang for soccer cleats.

Val looked down to see she was wearing only her new white socks. No shoes.

"I'll put my shoes on in the car!" Val answered, running

out behind Chloe and scooping up her indoor shoes on the way. Her socked feet felt the cold as soon as she hit the pavement dotted with snow and ice. Val hopscotched around the ice patches.

"You look like an uncoordinated frog," Chloe announced, holding open the door to the big black sedan.

"Yes, I do, *but* my socks are still dry!" Val said.

"You know, you could have just put your shoes on in the house. We would have waited for you."

Val smiled and shrugged. "Way more fun this way."

Chloe jumped in the back, and Val followed.

"Nice hopping" was the first thing Val heard. It was a boy's voice but certainly not Karl's.

Val looked to the front seat. Chloe's brother, Andrew, was smirking at Val. She was mortified. When Chloe said "we," Val thought she meant her and her driver, Karl. She'd had no idea anyone was watching her lurch down the sidewalk, much less Chloe's older brother, Andrew, a.k.a. Mr. Cool. Val had passed him in the halls at Chloe's house a few times but had never really talked to him. The way Mac had described him, you would have thought Andrew was a Malfoy wannabe in a Brookville letterman's jacket. Val sized Andrew up from the backseat. He certainly had Malfoy beat in the looks department. His hair was dark and on the longer side, sort of flopping across his forehead. He was looking down at his phone, so Val couldn't get a look at his eyes.

Val cocked her head toward Andrew and gave Chloe a look that said, "What gives?"

"Oh." Chloe shrugged. "Turns out that Brookville lacrosse has its games at the same place as our new field, so it works out great. Karl can drive us both at the same time, no problem."

"Yeah, great," Val answered quietly, putting it all together. She wasn't sure how she felt about going with Karl to practice several times a week. Something about being in Chloe's super-snazzy car made her feel uncomfortable. She also felt oddly relieved that her father wouldn't have to be part of the Breakers carpool.

"So did your blue-eyed wonder save the day?" Chloe asked. Val's love for Zarco was no secret.

"Yes!" Val yelled, and Andrew looked up suddenly. Val shrugged her shoulders and gave an awkward shrug.

"I can't believe he scored another game winner!" Chloe said.

Val was about to respond when Andrew said, "Actually, Mardirossian scored the goal." He held up his smartphone. Val peered closer and was surprised to see Andrew had been watching the game.

"Well, Zarco assisted," Val said.

"True, but they should never have been losing in the first place. They're cutting it awfully close, if you ask me."

Val hadn't asked, but she was impressed. She didn't want to admit it, but she agreed with him. Her favorite team was giving her high blood pressure lately. She couldn't even count the times the guys had had to score in the last seconds just to avoid a defeat or a tie.

"You watch soccer?" Val asked, unable to help herself. Most of the Brookville boys she knew only liked the big three: NBA, NFL, MLB.

"Our uncle lives in London," Andrew said by way of explanation.

"You like Man U?" she asked tentatively.

"I'm a Man City fan, actually. But I keep an eye on the competition," Andrew answered. Val contemplated this information. Manchester City and Manchester United were archrivals. Both teams came from the same city in the middle part of England. Val had heard that a Man City fan and a Man U fan couldn't even travel in the same car in England without coming to blows! Val settled into the backseat, unsure of what to say next. She decided it would be a good idea to get her shoes on while digesting this new information about Chloe's brother. She opened her bag to look for her shin guards. The bag tipped, and her old, ripped socks and the camouflage bandanna came spilling onto the seat. Val quickly tried to shove them back in.

"These are nasty," Chloe said, holding her nose and pointing at the old, dirty socks. She picked up the bandanna. "But...I still think this looks pretty cool."

Val got her shoes tied and grabbed the bandanna, this time tying it around her ankle. "How's this?"

"Even better," Chloe answered.

Val could see the parking lot for Total Sport. It was jammed with SUVs and helicopter parents, the ones who watched every minute of every practice as if they could will a clumsy kid some skills. They were the moms or dads who thought they knew more than the coaches, who screamed at the referees and generally embarrassed their kids.

Val was so relieved Miguel wasn't like that. Sure, he worried when she forgot her pants in twelve-degree weather, but to Val, that was just being a good parent. Rather than a helicopter parent, Val considered him more of a trampoline parent. He let her jump around like crazy but was ready to catch her in case she took a header down to the ground.

"Can I have Bubba, please?" Andrew said to the backseat in general.

Val glanced around for something that might fit the

bill. She saw Andrew turn back and thought he looked impatient. In the silence, she tried to come up with something witty. "Uh…Bubba? Where are you? I don't see any lost dudes back here."

Val could see a small grin flash across Andrew's face. Chloe laughed outright.

"Bubba is the name of his lacrosse stick," she said, rolling her eyes and picking it up from the floor of the backseat.

"Oh, right, of course," Val said with a chuckle. "Nice to meet you, Bubba. Sorry if I was stepping on your head!"

"Oh, Bubba's tough, don't worry," Andrew said from the front seat, patting the netting of the stick. "Not too many brains in there anyway."

"Seriously, your lacrosse stick has a name?" Val asked.

"Oh, yeah, this is Bubba. Webber is at home. He was a little under the weather. And Thor is retired. He won the league cup a few years back with a game winner."

"Ah, yes, I see," said Val.

"Have a good game, everyone," Karl said from the driver's seat. "Bubba, keep the fouls down."

Val, Chloe, and Andrew climbed out of the car and hustled into Total Sport, which resembled a chaotic airplane hangar. The sides of the building looked like a metal barn. They were red and massive, and the entrance was congested with throngs of parents and kids all trying to enter and exit at the same time through a revolving door designed to keep the cold air out. Bags, sticks, and balls clanged their way in and out of the building. Val was surprised when Andrew slowed the door and waited for her and Chloe to go first.

Through the crowds, Val saw the Breakers gathered on the closer field.

"I have to make a pit stop," Chloe said and headed to the bathroom. Val jogged over to Jessie, Jasmine, and Mac, who were passing the ball around.

"Hey, guys," Val said as she dropped her bag and bent down to check her laces and shin guards.

"Where'd you come from?" Jessie asked in a friendly tone that Val was happy to hear.

"I got a ride from Chloe, but the parking lot was totally jammed. She's in the bathroom."

Val carefully went through her pregame routine, including getting warm enough to do her important injury prevention stretches. Val had sprained her knee badly during the summer, and it had taken weeks to heal. The doctor said it was just dumb luck that she didn't tear a ligament. There was no injury more terrifying for a soccer player than a torn knee ligament.

"Don't take forever!" Mac teased.

Val had finished sticking her laces into the sides of her shoes when she heard someone calling her name.

She looked around and was surprised to see Andrew Gordon walking her way.

Puzzled, Val jogged over to meet him.

"What's up?" Val asked.

"Isn't this yours?" Andrew asked, holding out the bandanna.

"Oh, yeah, thanks. I guess it fell off."

"It was by the door. It's a zoo getting in here at change-over." He was right. When the exiting teams and the arriving teams all tried to jam through the door with their bags, it was chaos.

"Yeah, that was crazy." Val bent down to retie the cloth around her ankle. She was surprised to find Andrew still standing there. She looked up at him.

"Good luck in your game today," Andrew said.

"Yeah, you too," Val replied. "Have fun with Bubba."

"Oh, yeah. Bubba and I are gonna make some magic," Andrew said with a smile and then turned back to his field.

Val's eyes lingered on Andrew as he sauntered back toward the lacrosse field. He wasn't at all what she had expected. And, she noticed, he had really nice blue eyes.

"He's pretty cute, huh?" Ariana said, passing by.

Val shrugged and turned to rejoin her team. Jessie intercepted her.

"What was that all about?" she demanded.

Val was taken aback. "What was what all about?"

"What were you and Andrew Gordon talking about?"

"Nothing."

"I saw you, Val," Jessie said.

"We weren't talking. I dropped something. He was just giving it back to me."

"What, some ripped old socks?" Jessie asked.

"What are you talking about? What do you care?" Val finally said, exasperated.

Val hadn't seen Chloe jog over. "Care about what?"

Jessie didn't answer. Instead, she just turned away and in a fake voice said, "Oh, nothing. Come on, Chloe, let's pass."

Chloe shrugged her shoulders and grabbed her ball. Val scrunched up her face.

Drama.

5

eady?" Mac asked.

"Actually, yes. Believe it or not. I already checked my laces, did all my stretches, and checked my headband. Twice."

"Very impressive!" Mac said.

The two girls took to the field and started short one-touch passes, getting their bodies and minds ready to play. Val tried to shake off Jessie's behavior. She had to focus on the game.

"I've never heard of this team, El Fuego," Makena said after a stray pass went off to the side. "Have you?"

"Nope." Val backed up a few paces and sent Makena a high, loopy pass. Makena moved forward to take the ball out of the air, deftly bringing it down on her right foot. Val checked out the opposition. They were in bright, neon-orange uniforms with cool green-and-white-striped socks.

"I like their uniforms," Val said.

"Yeah, pretty cool." Makena sent a long ball back Val's way.

Looking closer, Val thought she recognized one of the El Fuego players. She had mid-length black hair, similar in color to Val's.

"I think that girl might go to my school," Val said, puzzled. "Or she used to. I think her name is Gabriela or something like that."

"Well, they look pretty good," Makena said, trapping a sharp pass from Val.

Val watched Gabriela and her teammates laugh as they played keep-away on their side of the field. A blue-and-white ball passed in front of her. It was Jessie's. By now, it was obvious Jessie was mad about something, but Val had no idea what. Val passed the ball back and turned her attention from her opponents to her teammate. She watched Jessie make a strong pass back to Chloe and then laughed when Chloe made an awkward trap. Well, Val thought, she looks pretty happy now. She just seems mad at me lately, especially today.

I better talk to her. This is silly. We're Soccer Sisters,

after all. We're friends. Plus we live by the Code. Code number three is very clear: Play with each other and don't take the fun out of it.

Soccer Sisters Team Code

1. Team first.
2. Don't be a poor sport or loser.
3. Play with each other and don't take the fun out of it.
4. Never put someone down if they make a mistake.
5. Practice makes perfect.
6. Never give up on the field or on one another.
7. Leave it on the field.
8. Always do the right thing.
9. Bring snacks on assigned days.
10. Beat the boys at recess soccer.

The Breakers had created the Code after all the drama in the summer: ten sacred rules to live by. Val loved the Code and had a copy on her bulletin board at home. When she felt confused about things—even outside of soccer— she looked at the Code rules she and her friends made up and did her best to follow them.

"Uh, hello?" Val heard Makena call from across the field. Val hadn't even noticed she was frozen on the spot, observing Jessie and forgetting she had the ball at her feet.

"Oh, sorry," Val said, sending a pass back to Mac. "I was just thinking."

"About?" Mac asked, coming closer.

Val knew that she should tell Makena about Jessie's mean behavior. It might not have been an official part of the Code, but it should be. Soccer Sisters didn't keep secrets. The referee blew the whistle indicating it was time for the girls to take the field.

"I'll tell you after the game," Val said. "It's no biggie."

"OK, don't forget. I have to leave right afterward to catch the end of Will's game," Makena said with a roll of her eyes. Will was Makena's younger brother, who, as it turned out, was becoming quite a little soccer star himself.

The girls took their spots on the field. Val promised herself she would find a way to talk to Jessie no matter what. As soon as the referee blew the whistle, Val could tell El Fuego was an excellent team. They started with the ball, passed it back, and kept control for what must have been a record for U13 girls' soccer. The ball went from the striker, a slight girl with amazing ball skills, to the midfield to the defense and back up again. Player to player, pass by pass, El Fuego moved the ball without the Breakers even getting a foot on it. Val and Makena were stunned, and all the Breakers were a little frustrated. It was embarrassing not to be able to even touch the ball! Luckily, El Fuego seemed happy to play keep-away and didn't do much attacking. After what felt like a long time, Jasmine was finally able to intercept a pass and get the Breakers in the game.

"Down the line!" Val heard Chloe yell, and she saw Chloe's long blond hair flapping behind her as she darted downfield. Makena had the ball at midfield and was looking for a pass. She gave the ball to Val, who immediately had two defenders on her. She tried to get the ball to Chloe, but it went out of bounds.

"*Hola,*" a girl said to Val as the two teams waited for Chloe to retrieve the ball.

"Uh, hi," Val answered. It was the girl she recognized from school.

"I'm Gabriela," she offered. "We used to have algebra together."

"Oh, right," Val said, feeling a little uncomfortable chatting in the middle of a game. A defender from Gabriela's team took the throw-in, and again El Fuego passed the ball around like they were practicing some kind of cone drill. And the Breakers were the cones. This time, however, they wasted no time attacking. Gabriela and her teammates moved the ball so beautifully that they got a shot off and past Ariana before most of the Breakers could even react.

"Let's go, girls!" Lily coached from the sideline. "Wake up out there! Val, less chatting, please!"

Val was mortified. Lily had seen her talking to the other team. What had she been thinking? Val moved into position, ready to even the score. Makena started with the ball, and this time it was the Breakers' turn to wow the crowd. Makena and Val moved forward in tandem, Val darting forward after every pass and Makena finding her feet every time. Chloe flanked them out wide, and Jasmine made a run to the far post.

"Drop!" Val heard Jessie call, which meant she wanted Val to pass the ball behind her. Val turned and got the ball to Jessie.

Jessie crossed it to Chloe, who first-timed it into the

box. Val and Makena both pounced. Val got there first, but defenders immediately surrounded her. Val flicked the ball with the outside of her left foot to Makena, who was in position to shoot. It was a perfect pass! Makena drilled the ball with her right foot, and just like that, the Breakers and El Fuego were tied 1 to 1.

Val and Makena hugged, and the rest of the Breakers ran over to give Mac a high-five.

"Hey, great cross," Val said to Jessie, offering her hand, but Jessie brushed past her and ran over to give Makena a hug.

"Seriously," Val muttered to herself. This was getting ridiculous.

"Hey, great pass," Gabriela said to Val as they got ready to restart.

Val wasn't used to her opponents handing out compliments. "Oh, thanks," Val said, thinking that El Fuego was a pretty nice team. Gabriela smiled, but then both girls put on their game faces and got back to work. Val really had to struggle to make anything happen during the rest of the game. It seemed like every time she got the ball, there were two defenders on top of her.

"Dude, they are all over me," Val said to Mac after the ball had gone out of bounds.

"They are," Makena agreed. "They must have scouted our team before the game or something."

Sure enough, the next time Val got the ball, she heard several of the El Fuego players yell something and realized they were talking about her in Spanish. A jolt of excitement and pride shot through her. Again, two defenders surrounded Val and sent the ball wide.

"What do you guys call me?" Val finally asked Gabriela.

"*La abeja*, of course," Gabriela answered with a smile.

"The bee?" Val laughed.

"*Sí*, you are fast, buzz around, and have a nasty sting," Gabriela said. "With the ball, of course."

Val was flattered. El Fuego thought enough about her as a player to give her a nickname and make sure defenders were on her at all times.

Val decided it was time to live up to her nickname. She knew that if two girls were assigned to cover her, then someone on her team would always be open. The key was to figure out who that was. Val decided that she would get the ball and hold on to it, drawing as many defenders to her until she could find the open Breaker.

El Fuego knew how to pass the ball. The Breakers were also good passers, but Val saw that passing was definitely something her team needed to work on. After a rare bad pass, Val stripped the ball from Gabriela at about midfield and broke free toward the goal. She could feel the defenders closing in on her as they had all game. Val held the ball close and protected it with her body while trying to look up and find the open player. Now she had three defenders on her. She moved quickly left and right, not really trying to get to the goal but just holding the ball long enough so that her team could get into scoring position.

"Now! Now! Now! Val!" she heard Mac call as she made a diagonal run in front of Val. Val fed her the ball and watched as she took off toward the goal. Val raced after Mac, keeping an eye on the last defender while being careful to stay onside. In soccer, the attacking players have to stay even with the last defender until the ball is kicked or else they're offside. It's a tough rule to learn, and even experienced players get called for a foul. For Val, getting caught offside was the worst mistake because it meant she wasn't paying attention or observing what was going on around her. When the linesperson saw a player offside, he or she raised a flag, the whistle blew, and the offending team would lose both the ball and its chance to score. It was downright embarrassing.

"Send it long, Mac!" Val called.

Makena sent a looping pass over the defense and Val

ran onto the ball, making sure she was not offside. No flag went up, and no whistle blew. Val gathered the ball at full sprint and crossed into the eighteen-yard penalty box. She was about to shoot when she felt a tug at her shirt. El Fuego was fast too, and they had caught up to her. The defender cut her off. Val juked left, but another orange shirt had come to help. She lifted her head to try to find Makena or Chloe. She was surrounded. Val pulled the ball back and realized she had no option but to dribble. Gabriela was next to try to stop her. One by one, Val outmaneuvered the El Fuego girls, bobbing and weaving until she found herself with a shot. Wasting no time, Val planted her left foot in the ground and did nearly a 180 to shoot the ball with her right. Her shot wasn't hard, but it didn't have to be. It was low and on target. The El Fuego goalie made a beautiful dive, arms outstretched, but she couldn't reach. Val's shot hit the side netting, and the whistle blew. Breakers 2, El Fuego 1. This win meant the Breakers would play for the indoor championship!

Val and her Soccer Sisters celebrated their goal while the El Fuego girls just shook their heads. Val thought she heard one of them mutter, "Unstoppable."

"Who needs Zarker!" Chloe teased. "Eat your heart out, Man U. We have our own superstar right here!"

"Zarco!" Val corrected, laughing. Out of the corner

of her eye, Val spied the Brookville lacrosse team watching the game and banging their sticks on the ground in approval. Val beamed. She hadn't intended to dribble through six players to score the game winner, but she'd been surrounded. The final whistle blew, and the Breakers cheered their hard-fought victory. The teams lined up to shake hands, and El Fuego's coach made a point of stopping Val in the line.

"You are a fantastic player, *señorita*," he said in a voice that sounded much like her father's.

"*Gracias*," Val answered instinctively.

Val stopped when she reached Gabriela. "You should come and kick around with us after school sometime, Val," Gabriela said. "We're even thinking of trying to get the school to start a team. We'd love to play with you anytime."

"Thanks," Val said, surprised at all the attention.

Lily shook hands with the coach from El Fuego. It was clear they knew each other.

"Girls, this is Juan Robertson. I played with his sister in college. To both teams, I just want to say this game was beautiful to watch. It's one of those days that someone ends up winning, but really all the girls on both teams should feel like winners. Days like today are the reason we love this sport."

Val lingered a little longer to talk with Juan and

Gabriela for a moment as the rest of the Breakers moved to the sidelines to gather their bags and coats.

"Val, let's go!" Chloe called. Val saw Chloe and her brother waiting by the exit.

Val hustled over, happy to see that Jessie was also nearby. "I'm coming!" Val said, picking up her bag.

"Hey, that was a nice piece of footwork," Andrew said as Val approached.

"Thanks," Val said. "They were all over me. I was trying to find someone to pass to but couldn't."

"Yeah, they were marking you really tight from the beginning of the game," Andrew said.

"I guess," Val answered, noting that this meant he'd been watching. "They were good."

"Where are they from?" Chloe asked. "I've never seen them."

"I guess they're a new team. Actually some of them are from my town, and some of them go to my school."

"Cool," Chloe said. "They were nice. OK, you ready?"

"Ready," Val said. The trio started walking to the door when Val remembered her pledge to track down Jessie and talk to Makena.

"Actually, guys, can you give me one second?" Val asked.

"OK," Chloe said, stopping by the entrance.

"Hey, Jessie!" Val called, running after her. "Wait up." Val jogged over, and Jessie turned around. "That was quite a game, huh?" Val said.

Jessie didn't answer right away but just glared at Val. "Looks like you knew some of them," she said finally. "Do you?"

"I guess I do. One of the girls used to be in my math class, I think. She's nice."

"Oh, you like them?" Jessie asked with a sneer.

"Yeah, why not? They were cool," Val said. "Jessie, is something the matter? It feels like you're mad at me. Did I do something?"

Jessie was quiet for a second.

"Actually, yes, Val," she said. "There is something wrong, and it's time you knew it. None of the girls are brave enough to tell you the truth, but I will."

"Tell me what?"

"Look, Val, you just don't belong on this team anymore. You don't go to our school. You don't live in our town."

"What are you talking about?" Val said, immediately angry. "Are you crazy?"

"Things have changed. You just don't see it. I mean, your dad doesn't really help with carpool, and even if he could, do you really think Chloe would be seen dead in that clunker he drives? And you're always late these days. I'm sorry to have to be the one to tell you, but everyone else is too scared to hurt your feelings."

Val felt like someone had punched her in the stomach. What was Jessie talking about? She looked around for Makena, realizing she had missed her. There was no way Jessie was speaking for her team, no way she was speaking for Mac. She looked for Chloe, who was waiting by the door. Val noticed she did actually look a little annoyed. Could what Jessie was saying really be true? The Breakers didn't want her anymore?

"No," Val said firmly. "You're making all this up. Come on, Jessie."

"I'm not, actually," Jessie fired back. "No one wants to hurt your feelings, but face it. You don't fit in anymore. Though you fit in fine with that team we played today."

Jessie gestured toward the remaining El Fuego players and delivered what felt to Val like a final, devastating blow: "Why don't you just go play with them?"

6

Val half walked, half stumbled back to the car. She felt like a passenger on an amusement park ride, the serious ones you have to be taller than fifty-four inches to ride. Maybe sign a puke waiver. She felt Six Flags–sick to her stomach.

Chloe laughed when she saw her, probably thinking she was doing the goofy frog walk again. "Let's get out of here," she said as Val collapsed in the roomy backseat.

Val only nodded. Jessie had rendered her speechless. She'd launched her verbal grenade, flashed a fake sympathetic look, and walked away. Just like that. Val knew Jessie was full of it, totally and utterly mean and crazy—and wrong. Val tried to calmly consider what Jessie had said, but then another wave of OMG hit her right in the belly.

"Oh, turn it up, Karl!" Chloe cried when she heard the new Katy Perry song on the radio. "I love this one."

Andrew rolled his eyes and grinned at Val as Chloe danced around in the backseat. Val tried to return his warm smile, but all her game happiness had been wiped away like snowflakes on a windshield. Val wanted to talk to Chloe, but the music was too loud. Chloe, oblivious, bopped from side to side, trying to get Val to dance with her. Val's glazed eyes wandered around the plush car, complete with driver, and she realized she'd been blind. She imagined what Chloe would say in her father's old, junky car, a giant hole in the floor, recipes everywhere. She wouldn't *say* anything, of course. Jessie was right about that. Val knew that Chloe was too nice. But she saw now that Chloe probably felt sorry for her. Val didn't belong in this fancy car with a driver. It made her feel like a fake. She needed to escape. She tried to think of the Code but came up empty. She really needed to talk to Makena.

"Hey, want to come over?" Chloe yelled over the radio. "We can make up some dances or something."

"Oh, thanks," Val answered. "But actually if you can just drop me at Mac's, my dad's going to pick me up there later."

Chloe turned her head and frowned. "I thought Mac had to go to her brother's game."

"Oh, yeah, she did," Val said, realizing her mistake. "But…my dad was doing something in their kitchen."

Chloe gave Val a quizzical look but shrugged and said, "OK. No problemo."

Val made sure all her old socks and bandannas and worn shoes were well contained in her soccer bag and then scurried from the car as soon as it came to a stop. For the first time, she was embarrassed that her father worked for the family of one of her teammates.

"Bye, Val," Andrew said.

She waved a quick and confident good-bye and ran up the front walk to the Walshes' door. She rang the doorbell and pulled her jacket closed, praying there was actually someone home.

The big black car idled in front of the house. Karl was, of course, waiting to make sure Val got inside. Val rang the doorbell again. She peered through the little glass windows on either side of the front door. *Oh, please, someone be home*, she pleaded silently. Val was banking on the fact that the entire Walsh family almost never went to Makena's or Will's games.

The tinted window of the black car smoothly rolled down.

"Are you sure someone's home?" Andrew asked from the passenger seat.

"Uh, yeah," Val stammered, banging harder on the door.

"OK," Andrew said, but Val could tell by the look on his face that he was unconvinced.

Finally, Val heard a noise on the other side of the door. She raised her fist to knock one more time, but the door finally swung open, and Papa, Makena's grandfather, unleashed a tirade in Italian.

Val couldn't understand anything he was yelling and thought she caught him muttering something about Final Jeopardy. But it didn't matter because he wasn't looking for conversation anyway. He just turned around and walked back to his den, leaving Val alone in the entry. Val could hear the television blaring. No wonder no one could hear the doorbell or Val's knocking. Val waved to Andrew, Karl, and Chloe and closed the door.

"Makena?" Val called as she reached the bottom of the stairs. "Anyone home?"

In anyone else's house, it might have felt weird to be left unaccompanied by a cranky grandfather, but Val loved the Walshes' home. She'd been hanging out there almost all her life. And whereas Chloe's enormous mansion was perfect and spotless and modern, Makena's house just felt familiarly funky. There were piles of life—papers, permission slips, recipes, and food and nature magazines—stacked on the kitchen counter. There were bowls of fruit on the table and usually something good cooking on the stove. The Walshes' house was a home, and just being there already helped Val feel a little better.

"Hi, Val!" a voice called from the top of the stairs. It was Makena's mom, Stacey. "Your father already finished fixing the stove. He went back to Rosa's."

"Oh. I was actually looking for Makena. Is she home yet?" Val asked hopefully, dropping her soccer bag on the floor.

"Actually, she's not. She's at her brother's game, if you can believe it."

Val smiled. She'd always had a soft spot for Will.

"She'll be home soon," Makena's mom said, turning to go back upstairs. "Make yourself comfortable. Papa is watching TV in the den. Just be careful you don't talk to him during Final Jeopardy."

Val tried to laugh, but her heart wasn't it in. It felt heavy in her chest. All she mustered was a thin smile.

"Val?" Makena's mom asked. "Is everything all right? Did you guys lose today?"

Val wanted to tell her everything, but something—a weird feeling—clamped her mouth shut. She forced herself to stand up straighter, lifted her chin, and put on her best fake smile.

"Oh, everything is great! We won today," she said as

perkily as she could, but still she heard the glumness in her voice.

"Are you sure you're OK?" Mrs. Walsh asked. "How's the knee?"

"It's fine," Val said reassuringly. She knew better than to get Makena's mom going. She didn't need any starter fuel to worry.

Mrs. Walsh tilted her head to the side and looked down at Val. *Uh-oh. She knows me too well*, Val thought. "Why don't you get yourself a snack and then come up and help me while you wait for Makena?" she asked Val. "I'm doing a special on the medical uses of honey."

"Sure, that sounds fun, actually."

After walking into the kitchen, Val decided to skip the snack and made her way upstairs.

Mrs. Walsh was in her home office, which was packed with butterflies, crickets, beetles, wasps, spiders, ants, termites, scorpions, and pretty much any other kind of weird bug you could imagine. Makena's mom was one of the world's foremost experts on bugs. She had her own web show called *Madame Butterfly's Journey*. Val watched as Mrs. Walsh organized her supplies for the show. She had several display cases with various-size bees. She also had a wide array of honeys on the table, and Val noticed that there was a good-size bandage wrapped around Mrs. Walsh's right hand.

"Did you cut yourself?" she asked.

"Yes, actually, I did. So silly. I was working in the yard, without gloves, and I reached down and scratched the top of my hand pretty badly." She lifted up her hand to show Val. "It's the reason I'm doing this show on bees."

Val was confused. "What do bees have to do with your hand?"

"Well, when I reached down, I scratched my hand against a sharp rock and got two really serious gashes on the top of my hand. They weren't deep enough for stitches, but they were pretty bad. The weird thing was they were about exactly the same size. So I decided to do a little experiment." Slowly, she began to unravel the white gauze. "So you know that honey bees make honey, right?"

Val nodded.

"Well, bacteria cannot survive in honey. It's just too thick. Too sugary. It also fights infection. So for thousands of years people have covered their wounds with honey. The ancient Egyptians used honey as a wound treatment as early as 3000 BC, and it's even been found in Egyptian tombs."

This was news to Val. "Seriously? I put honey on my

toast. Or if I have a sore throat, my dad gives me hot water with lemon and honey."

"Right, when you drink hot water with honey, the thick, sugary honey can make your throat hurt less. Some honey is also thought to have antibacterial properties."

Val tried to get a better look at Mrs. Walsh's hand. It looked like a regular old bandage.

"So you put honey on your cut?"

Mrs. Walsh nodded. "I did. On one of them I put honey, and on the other cut I put an antibiotic lotion. The regular old kind you get at the pharmacy."

"And you want to see which one got better faster?" Val asked.

"Bingo," Mrs. Walsh said.

"Have you peeked?" Val asked.

Mrs. Walsh smiled. "Well, of course I have to change the bandage every day to keep it clean."

"So you just smeared honey into your cut?" Val was appalled. That really did seem awfully messy.

Makena's mom laughed. "No, no. You definitely want to use sterilized honey specially made for wound care."

"Does the queen bee make all the honey?" Val asked.

"Actually the queen bee doesn't make honey at all. She

lays eggs. Up to three thousand a day. The workers make the honey from flower nectar. It's their food."

"Seriously?"

"Yep." Mrs. Walsh turned and picked up a small glass case. "Here I have a specimen of a queen honey bee and a worker bee." She handed the case to Val.

The queen bee was much longer than the worker, Val could see. "This is so cool," she whispered. "How do you get to be the queen?"

"Well, the queen is just a regular bee that's fed royal jelly. That's what makes her turn into a queen."

"Wow, this is totally freaky stuff," Val said.

"This is just nature," Makena's mother replied.

Val was fascinated and couldn't wait for Mrs. Walsh to remove her bandage so they could see which one of her cuts was healing faster. Val was betting on the bees.

A door slammed downstairs, followed immediately by what sounded like a herd of buffalo bounding up the stairs and then yelling, "Mom! We're home! Mom!"

Mrs. Walsh's and Val's eyes met. "Mac's home," they said together, both with a smile.

"Can you wait until Makena comes up to take off the rest of the bandage?" Val asked excitedly.

"Sure," Mrs. Walsh replied. Spontaneously, Val jumped

up and gave her a quick hug. She had totally forgotten about all the drama at soccer and felt suddenly so grateful to Makena's mother. She couldn't wait to share the experience with her friend.

"Makena!" Val cried, heading down the hall. "You gotta come see this!"

7

"Hey! I didn't know you were coming over. What's up?" Makena asked, coming up the stairs. She was still in her uniform from the game.

"Oh, you gotta see this stuff! Your mom is doing the coolest—" A blur of blondish-red hair, orange uniform, and nine-year-old energy came barreling past Makena.

"Hey! Watch it!" Makena yelled as her brother, Will, pushed her to the side.

"*Mom! Mom! Mom!*" Will screamed. Val pressed her back against the wall to get out of the way.

"*Mom! I scored the game winner today!*"

Makena rolled her eyes at Val and said, "Beyond annoying."

Val laughed. Will was pretty entertaining most of the time, but she knew that he drove Makena crazy. She liked to call him her "little bother." Val was an only child and had always been a little envious that Makena had a brother. Mac always had someone to hang out with. Val would have loved to have a sister or brother, even if he was a bother.

"How was his game?" Val asked.

"Oh, it was regular nine-year-old soccer. Bunching up and stealing the ball from each other. At least Will knows better than that."

"Did he score the game winner, really?" Val asked.

"Yeah. It wasn't a bad goal, but now he thinks his name is Will Messi or something. Like he was the first person in the world to score a goal."

Val definitely heard a little jealousy in her friend's voice. Makena did not like sharing the soccer spotlight with her brother. Val tried to imagine Will as the next Lionel Messi, the Argentine left-footer who played for Barcelona and was considered perhaps the greatest soccer player of all time.

"The next Messi?" Val joked. "Maybe Nike will name a line of soccer shoes after him sometime soon?"

"Exactly," Makena said, heading down the hallway. "With a big orange stripe like his crazy hair!"

Makena stopped in front of her mom's office and waved. Val could hear Will telling his mother the play-by-play of his goal. Val couldn't admit it to Makena, but she was happy for Will. For so long, Makena was the only member of the Walsh family to get all the praise for her soccer playing. Makena stomped away.

"She didn't even ask me about my game!" Makena said, clearly put out.

"Oh, I already told her we won," Val said quickly, hoping to appease her friend.

"What did you want to show me before?" Makena asked, opening the door to her bedroom.

"Oh, your mom is doing totally cool stuff with honey and bees," Val told her. "It's kind of awesome."

"Oh, right. Putting the honey on her cut or something weird like that?" Makena asked, bored.

"Yeah, it's so cool."

Makena gave Val a look that made it clear she did not think it was cool at all. "My mom and her bugs." She rolled her eyes again. "Let's go hang out in my room."

Val followed Makena into her room. Posters of famous soccer players were plastered all over the wall: Abby Wambach. Alex Morgan. Ronaldo. Messi. Val had most of the same ones in her bedroom too, although Val's room was about one-quarter the size. She flopped on the bed and watched as Makena took off her shoes, socks, and shin guards. Val was dying to hear Makena say that Jessie was out of her mind. That she had no idea what she was talking about. But Val also realized that she hadn't been able to talk to Makena about all of Jessie's weird behavior lately. It was like Val was the only one who was noticing. She didn't know where to start.

"Hey, Mac, remember before the game when I said there was something I wanted to talk about?"

"Oh, right," Makena said. "What's up?"

Val searched for the right words. Even in her mind, Jessie's claim that they didn't want her on the team anymore sounded dumb and impossible. She didn't even want to say it out loud. But she knew she could talk to Makena. Makena was her best friend in the world. Makena was her Soccer Sister. Makena was her family. They shared everything.

"Well, it's just that lately, Jessie—" Just as she was about to spit the words out, Makena's door burst open like a Navy SEAL raid.

"Where are my headphones?" Will demanded, filling the room in an instant. "You had them last."

"Will you get out of my room?!" Makena barked at her brother as he rummaged through her desk, opening drawers and shoving piles of papers and clothes onto the ground.

"Give me my headphones and I'll leave," Will said. He moved from the desk to the dresser.

"Stop touching all my stuff!" Makena yelled. "I don't have your stupid headphones."

"What's this?" Will held up a piece of clothing. "Is this a bra?" He cracked up.

"Yes, it's a sports bra, you moron," Makena fumed.

Val tried to help. "Will, I think I saw your headphones in the front entry," she said, hoping he would leave before Makena went nuclear. No luck.

"What the heck is this?" Will was in Makena's closet now. "Is this some kind of Halloween costume?"

Will emerged from the closet with a dress on a hanger. Attached to the hanger was a pair of shoes with a small heel!

"Put that down!" Makena screamed.

"Since when are you prom queen?" Will asked with a sour face. Clearly, he didn't approve of Makena's dress. "You trying out for a Disney Princess job or something?" Will did a fake parade wave, and Val stifled a laugh.

"It's my dress for the Snow Fairy Dance. Get your dirty hands off it." Makena went over to wrestle the hanger out of his hands. The dress was pale yellow and made of flowing layers. The shoes matched perfectly. Val had never seen Makena with anything like it.

"Wow!" Val said, almost unintentionally. It was one of the most beautiful dresses she had ever seen.

Makena grabbed the hanger and shoved her brother roughly out the door as he began humming the theme from *Frozen*. Makena slammed the door shut, turned around, and began to smooth out the dress.

"You like it?" Makena asked shyly.

"It's awesome," Val said honestly. "Are those matching shoes?"

Makena nodded and flashed a radiant smile. Val could tell she was excited.

"Where did you get it?"

"The mall," Makena said.

"You and your mom?"

"No, I went with Chloe and Jessie," Makena said, putting the dress back into her closet. "Jessie spotted it in this tiny store. She said it went with my freckles."

Val had no idea Makena had had an outing with Jessie and Chloe. She felt rotten. Not only was she not invited, she hadn't even known about it. Something else felt weird too, but she couldn't put her finger on what it was.

"You bought a dress before you asked someone to the dance?" Val asked.

"Oh, no, I got it afterward," Makena answered.

Val was confused. Did this mean Makena had asked a boy to the Snow Fairy Dance?

"You asked someone?" Val was scared to hear the answer.

"Yeah," Makena answered casually. "I asked that kid from homeroom, Justin. It wasn't that big a deal after all. Some girls are freaking out, so I decided to just get it over with. Right in the morning. I told you, right?"

Val didn't answer right away. She was trying to calculate what she was hearing. Trying to figure out what it all meant. Makena Walsh, her best friend in the world, tomboy extraordinaire, had asked a boy to a dance, shopped for a dress, and Val knew nothing about any of it.

"Yeah, yeah." Val played it off. "I'm sure."

Val watched as Makena carefully hung the dress back in her closet. Val thought back to what Jessie had said at the game. Maybe she wasn't making it all up. Maybe that's what Makena, Chloe, and Jessie had talked about at the mall when they were shopping.

Something on the ground caught Val's eye. It was a long black cord with a pointed silver tip. Val grabbed the cord and started to pull. Something bulky started to emerge from under the bed. Val knew immediately what it was: Will's headphones.

"Look what I found," Val said, holding them up.

"Chuck 'em in the garbage," Makena suggested.

"I'll bring them to him," Val said. She was happy for the distraction. She'd been so certain that Jessie was dead wrong, but now the queasiness of doubt had returned. She needed to clear her head and then talk to Makena.

Val exited Makena's bedroom in search of Will.

"Oh, there you are, Val," Mrs. Walsh called out as Val passed her office. "Did you still want to see my big reveal? Did you tell Makena?"

Val stopped walking. She stood in the hallway, holding Will's headphones, feeling lost in a familiar place.

"I told Makena, but…" Val felt shy about finishing the sentence. Mrs. Walsh finished it for her.

"She wasn't interested?"

Val shrugged. Mrs. Walsh flashed a knowing smile. "Don't worry, Val. Lately, Makena's been a little distracted. She used to be mommy's little helper, but now she thinks my work is boring," Mrs. Walsh said, chuckling to herself.

"She said that?" Val asked.

"Oh, no, of course not. She's growing up. Both of you girls are. Interests change, and I understand. She still pretends like she's interested, but I know she's not." Makena's mom paused for a moment. "Honestly, Val, I think she just doesn't want to hurt my feelings."

Val's head began to spin. She dropped the headphones on the ground.

"Val? Are you OK?" Mrs. Walsh asked.

"Uh," she stammered, "I just remembered something I was supposed to do."

"Val, what's the matter?" Mrs. Walsh asked, getting up from her chair.

"I gotta go!" Val turned and barreled down the stairs, flung open the front door, and started to run.

8

Val ran. She sprinted through the frigid streets of Brookville. The leafless trees were a blur through her tear-filled eyes. Manicured lawns and fancy houses for big families flooded Val's peripheral vision, further proof of her outsider status. She sprinted for another few blocks and suddenly felt a twinge in her knee. She knew she should slow down but couldn't. She needed to feel the burn in her muscles. Maybe if her legs hurt, her heart wouldn't.

She. Doesn't. Want. To. Hurt. My. Feelings. The words pounded in Val's head each time her feet hit the pavement. She turned away from town and up the hill. She felt another sharp pain in her knee. The orthopedist had told her to always warm up before she ran, but in this moment she didn't care. She felt her whole world slipping away from her, and if she couldn't be a Soccer Sister, what did her knee matter anyway? She pushed herself up a steep hill, her heart thudding. Flashes of her team, of her friends, of Makena and Chloe, of her coach, filled her vision. Jessie's words ricocheted through her mind. She saw a car approaching and slowed, veering to the right side of the road. She didn't notice the slick and icy gravel. The black ice. She was still wearing her indoor soccer shoes, which had no traction. As the car passed, Val's feet went out from under her. She tumbled, falling hard to the ground in a heap. Her hands were scraped and bloodied. She felt something pull in her leg and twist in her knee.

The car passed. She lay by the side of the road unnoticed, heaving, hurting, and defeated. The girl who would never give up on the field was ready to give up on the game. Her exhausted body didn't yet feel the cold winter air. Her hands stung, and her knee ached, but a memory began to fill her mind. Her very first soccer game. Before travel soccer. Before she was a Breaker. Or a Soccer Sister. The first team she ever played on was part of a recreational league, where little six-year-old girls played against other six-year-old girls from the same town. Val struggled to remember the name of the team. She could see their bright-yellow uniforms and remembered how insanely excited and proud she and Mac were to be able to put them on for the very first time.

The day of that first game was a different kind of memory. Sharper and brighter than most. Fewer images than feelings. A real uniform. Val was part of a team. She and Makena were on the *same* team. How could it get any better? She knew her father must have arranged that. Val remembered struggling to pull up her tube socks and get her shin guards in place. Forget tying her shoes. She hadn't even learned how to do that yet. Her dad did that for her too. They played that first game in the spring. It was chilly but sunny. Most of the game was just a bunch of little girls chasing the ball in a giant pack. These were the days before passing and teamwork; soccer was nothing more than the disorganized, joyful exuberance of six-year-old energy.

She could still remember the feeling of running down the tiny field with her only mission: get that ball. Their coach was a woman named Laura. She was kind and smart and a really good soccer player. She coached them gently but firmly, guiding them in a no-nonsense way. Val liked that she never treated the players like babies. She taught them seriously, so they learned to take the game seriously. At least some of them did. A few lost ones were always picking at the grass and doing cartwheels across the goal.

Val still could remember how Coach Laura tried to

break soccer down into the most simple of ideas: be safe on defense, be in control in the midfield, and take chances on offense. Soccer was simple.

Val sighed. *When did everything change?* she wondered.

"The Daffodils!" Val suddenly said out loud to no one. All the girls' teams were named after flowers: the Daffodils, the Tiger Lilies, the Clovers. Val also remembered that she, Makena, and the Daffodils had lost that very first game by a ridiculously high score. Six to five or something like that. Coach Laura told them they had learned a very important lesson that day about defense and maybe they should start playing some. Val smiled at the memory.

"The Daffodils," she said again. She sat up and rubbed her knee. Out of the corner of her eye, she noticed someone standing nearby, watching her.

"I don't think daffodils are quite in bloom yet, Val." It was Andrew Gordon.

He was standing on the hill with a bemused look on his face. He had Bubba in one hand and a large red bag slung over his shoulder. Val had no idea how long he had been watching her.

"Uh…" Val stammered, totally at a loss for what to say. "Yeah. Uh. Actually I was just thinking about something."

Andrew tilted his head to the side and grinned. "Do

you always lie by the side of the road in a pile of leaves in the middle of winter to do your 'thinking'?" he asked.

Val couldn't help but laugh. She was covered in twigs and mud. She brushed them off and started to get up, wincing as pain shot through her upper leg. "Ouch," she said, involuntarily clutching at her knee.

Andrew moved quickly to help her. "Are you OK?" he asked, laying his lacrosse bag and stick down by the side of the road.

Val's first instinct was to say she was fine, to pretend there was nothing wrong. But she wasn't very good at hiding her feelings. Plus he did kind of find her muttering to herself by the side of the road. So instead, she just told him the truth. "Well, I'm having a kind of awful day," Val said, her voice cracking slightly. "I tried to run to forget about it all, and then I slipped and fell and hurt my leg. So no, I guess I'm not OK. I'm kind of a mess right now."

Andrew nodded in agreement and then moved closer to offer his arm. He too slipped on the ice.

"Whoa," he said, steadying himself.

"It's pretty slick," Val offered with a weak chuckle. "Black ice. It got me."

"I see that," Andrew said. "Hang on a second." He reached back and grabbed his long lacrosse stick.

"Bubba, at your service," he said with a wobbly bow. He passed Bubba to Val, and she grabbed it, lacing her fingers into the basket where the ball goes. He held it steady until she got past the ice and onto the road. He held her up by the arm as they stood on the steep hill.

"Thanks," Val said sincerely. "I might have stayed there all day."

"No problem. But we better get out of the middle of the road. People come flying down this hill all the time," Andrew said. "Where are you headed?"

Val really didn't know. She shrugged. "I guess I'll just walk, uh, limp, into town."

"That works," Andrew replied. "I'm going to practice some shooting at the school. I didn't have a very good game today. I'll walk with you."

Val and Andrew maneuvered down the hill carefully. Val's knee was still sore, but she felt like it was stable enough to walk on.

"So is that the same knee you hurt in the tournament last summer?" Andrew asked as they reached the bottom of the hill.

"Yeah, it is. I thought I had torn my ACL, but I was lucky. It was a bad sprain, not a tear," Val said.

"I hear about a lot of athletes blowing out their knees," Andrew said sympathetically.

"I know. It's awful. How did you know I hurt my knee last summer?"

"Oh, my sister told me. She's obsessed with your team. It's, like, the only thing she wants to talk about."

"Really?" she asked. Val was surprisingly happy to hear this.

"Yeah. I pretend not to listen, but I know what's going on," Andrew said with a laugh. "And by the way, last I saw you, uh, like two hours ago, you had just scored the game winner in an awesome match. That's not too awful a day, if you ask me."

Val knew he must want to know how she went from glory to gutter in a matter of hours. She felt bad that she hadn't even asked about his game. She sighed and tried to explain. "There's just been some stuff going on with my team off the field that's getting to me."

Andrew nodded his understanding. "My whole basketball team fell apart this winter because a few parents got into an argument over something dumb. One minute you're a team, and another minute, a disaster. It's scary how fragile it can be sometimes."

They walked in silence toward town. Val's progress was slow, but despite the cold, Andrew never complained or rushed her. He also didn't seem to mind when Val stayed quiet. She was grateful that he didn't push her to explain more. Not that she could. Her emotions were as jumbled as a scattered deck of cards. Somehow talking to him was calming her down.

They approached town, and Val felt herself slow down, but it had nothing to do with her knee. She didn't want her time with Andrew to end. She felt like she could talk to him about anything. Like he somehow already understood.

"Have you ever had a friend that just changed on you? For no reason?" she blurted out.

"Actually, yes. You know Moose?" Andrew asked.

"Moose?" Val asked.

"Oh, sorry," Andrew said with a chuckle, "Matthew George. Everyone calls him Moose."

"I don't think so."

"Oh, he's really tall and quiet, and his hair kind of sticks up after he takes off his helmet…anyway, I took his starting spot at a lax tournament, and he got all weird with me after that even though I had nothing to do with the decision. We still play on the same teams, but we just don't hang out anymore. You can't really be best friends with everyone, I guess."

They walked for a few more minutes in comfortable silence as Val thought about what Andrew had said about Moose.

"Well, I turn here," Andrew said, gesturing to the school fields behind him. "Are you sure you're OK?"

Val knew she didn't have to pretend. "Yeah, I'll be fine," she said. "A little rest, a little ice, I'll be good as new."

"I meant with the team stuff," Andrew said.

"I'm trying to figure it out," Val said. "Thanks for the hand. Uh, I mean the stick."

"Bubba and I are happy to help anytime."

Val turned to go.

"Uh, Val?" Andrew called to her. She turned slowly around.

"Yeah?"

"You're not what I expected," he said.

Val lifted her eyes to his. "You're not what I expected either. You're actually pretty cool. For a Man City fan."

Andrew laughed. "I'll see you around."

Val waved and turned to go, but then Andrew called to her again.

"Val?" he said, stepping closer. "Hold on a minute."

"Yeah?" she asked, noticing again the blueness of his eyes. Kind of like the ocean just offshore. Andrew came closer, his arm reaching slowly behind her. Val froze.

Andrew leaned in, and his hand touched the back of her head. He pulled out a stick and said, "Hey, Man U girl. You have a giant pile of leaves and a huge stick in your hair."

9

Val was walking toward town, still picking twigs out of her hair, when she heard the familiar rumble. It sounded like a cross between a lawn mower and a hair dryer, only not quite as powerful. Her dad's clunker.

Miguel pulled up alongside her.

"*M'ija*," he said with a sigh. *M'ija* was what he always called her. "My daughter," it meant. It was a term of endearment, a sweet nickname, or sometimes, as he said it now, an expression of exasperation.

"*Por favor, niña. ¿Dónde estabas?*" Miguel asked. Val turned to the car. Of course he wanted to know where she'd been. She was supposed to be at the restaurant right after the game. Hours ago.

"Did Makena's mom call you?" Val asked, feeling guilty.

"*Sí. Y Makena. Y Chloe*," Miguel said. He was speaking

to her only in Spanish, which Val knew meant he was tired, worried, or mad.

Miguel suddenly noticed there was a scrape on Val's hand and that her pants were covered with mud. She was shivering.

"*¿Qué pasó? Cuéntame.*"

He wanted to know what happened. *Oh, everything,* Papi, she thought. Suddenly, Val was hit by a black wave of emotion. It was all too much. Too many feelings. Too many complications. Her leg hurt. She was cold. She was really, really tired. Val wished she could just be a little girl again and fold up into her father's arms. She started to cry. Tears welled up in her eyes. They streamed down her cheeks, and she sobbed a giant "Papi!"

Val didn't often cry. They both knew that. Miguel's anger immediately turned to concern, and he pulled the car to the side, got out, and ran to embrace her.

"*No llores, hija mía, no llores,*" Miguel said, stroking her hair, plucking out the last of the leaves. Val allowed him to guide her to the car. The tears continued to flow. Tears for her bruised heart and her splintered pride. He held her. He didn't ask any questions. He stroked her head and kissed her tears. When finally she calmed down, he found an old T-shirt from the backseat and wiped her face. She shook her head and laughed a little: her dad and his car full of random junk.

"We should talk a little, no?" her father asked gently. Val nodded, getting into the front seat. Miguel put the car into drive and made a sharp U-turn, away from town but not toward home.

"Where are we going?" she asked, confused.

Miguel rolled his eyes, as if she should already know. "*A los* World's Most Incredible Hot Dogs, *por supuesto.*"

Now Val really started to laugh. That fragile laugh after a good cry. Her father, the talented chef, food expert, Mexican by birth and blood, was obsessed with American hot dogs. He loved them. He loved the toppings. He loved to examine the casings. He had opinions on sauerkraut. He had conducted taste tests and ultimately deemed World's Most Incredible Hot Dogs in the Ridgeway Mall the best ever. The warmed, buttery buns were the deciding factor. Val adored the way he always said "incredible" with an exaggerated Spanish accent—*in-cre-dee-blay*—and the fact they always went there to eat when there were important family matters to discuss.

The mall was buzzing as Val and Miguel walked toward the restroom so she could wash her hands. She told her father her knee was feeling better. Still sore but functioning well enough. They passed the electronics kiosk, a Gap, and then a small boutique that caught Val's eye. There were several girls her age loitering out front. She didn't recognize them, but one was wearing a Brookville track T-shirt, so she figured they must attend Makena's school. Val smiled at the girls, who were texting and oohing and ahhing over a pair of platform pumps. Val slowed as she passed the shop. Her usual wardrobe consisted of comfy leggings and soccer jerseys, but seeing the dress in Makena's closet made her linger for a moment longer. Is this where Makena had come shopping? Without her?

Val meandered closer to the boutique, whose doors opened up to the mall with racks of dresses and tops right out front. She stopped to touch the fabric on a navy-blue dress. It was covered in tiny pieces of shimmering silk cutouts shaped like butterflies. The fabric felt fancy, and the butterflies floated on the dress as if in midair. The dress looked elegant and whimsical all at once, grown-up but not too old. Val thought it was kind of in between.

Like her.

"*¿Te gusta?*" Miguel asked. Val had forgotten he was even there.

"Yes," Val answered. "It's beautiful."

"*¡Vamos a comprarlo!*" Miguel said, happy to do anything to cheer up his daughter.

Val smiled but shook her head. "No, *gracias*. What do I need a dress like that for? Come on. Let's go eat."

They found a quiet table in the back, and Val unloaded her troubles on her father as he loaded toppings on his three hot dogs.

Yes, three: (1) traditional with sauerkraut and yellow mustard, the all-time favorite; (2) with onions cooked in ketchup (the smell of this one made Val want to hurl); and (3) *a la Mexicano*, his own creation, a footlong with hot sauce, raw onions, cilantro, and a touch of lime.

Val shook her head as mustard dribbled down her father's chin.

"OK," Miguel said, "*Cuéntame todo.*"

He wanted to know everything. Val told him about how annoyed she was that her teammates were so obsessed with the Snow Fairy Dance. She told him how Jessie had been being mean to her at practices and she had no idea why. She told him how she'd tried to talk to Makena but feared Makena just didn't want to hurt her feelings. She told him how she'd run to escape and fallen and how Andrew Gordon had helped her up and walked her to town.

Miguel seemed relieved. At least nothing terrible had happened when she was running through town. He put down the onion hot dog and said, "*Pero*, what could anyone say that could upset you so much?"

Val hesitated just a little. She felt the tears coming back. "Jessie said that they didn't want me on the team anymore, that Makena and Chloe didn't want to hurt my feelings, but that things had changed."

"But, Val, you know this is not true. Did you talk to Mac? She is…*como tu hermana*."

"I tried, Papi."

"Did she say this too?" Miguel asked with a shocked look on his face.

"No, she didn't say it, but…"

"But, *nada. M'ija*, you must have more faith in your friend."

Val hung her head a little bit. He was right. Why was she doubting her friends?

"Papi…" Val continued. "We played against a team called El Fuego. They were *Mexicanas*, like me. They were so nice. They were really good too. Some of them go to my school. A really cool girl named Gabriela."

"Ah, *te llamo una Gabriela hoy*," Miguel said, holding a finger in the air, making the connection.

"Gabriela called me today?" Val asked.

"*Sí*. She invited you to play with her after school. In the gym."

Val nodded. "I think they might start a school team."

"*Bueno*," Miguel nodded, liking the sounds of Gabriela.

"Papi, Jessie told me that I should go play with El Fuego."

"*¿Cómo?*" Miguel wanted to make sure he understood.

"She told me that I didn't belong on the Breakers anymore."

"*¿Y por qué?*"

Val shrugged.

Miguel pushed his final hot dog aside. He spoke slowly and carefully in English. "You must ask yourself why this girl has upset you so much." Val knew he was right. Miguel continued in Spanish. "I have always worried that this day might come. That you might want to play on a different team from Makena. That you might want to play in your own town. The Breakers are a wonderful team. Wonderful people. Maybe not this Jessie though. It has always been your decision to play soccer. You are so talented. Maybe it's not a bad idea to give something new a try?"

Val shook her head. "But, Papi, I am a Soccer Sister."

Miguel raised his eyebrows. "Maybe Gabriela is also a Soccer Sister. *Una hermana nueva.*"

10

Val and geometry were not friends. At least not at the moment. Tonight's torture was equilateral, isosceles, and scalene triangles. Generally, Val loved math, but on this evening she was having a hard time getting her thoughts together. Sitting alone at the big wooden table in the back of Rosa's, surrounded by books, she mindlessly tapped her pencil on the table. Tap. Tap. Tap. *OK, let me try this one more time*, Val thought. She refocused her eyes on the page and read aloud, "An equilateral triangle has three equal sides. An isosceles triangle has two equal sides, and a scalene triangle are all offside."

She copied it down and read it again. She took a closer look and groaned.

"Offside?" she shouted. "Unequal sides, not offside! Ugh!" Val tossed her pencil across the room.

The truth was Val could not get her mind off her team. She slammed her book shut in frustration. Her father had insisted she skip practice tonight to give her knee a rest. Val didn't resist. For the first time ever, she needed a break from her team. She'd called her coach to let her know she wasn't going to be there. But now she was feeling adrift. She hadn't played soccer all week, hadn't talked to Makena. She missed her team, and she had to admit, she had been looking forward to seeing Andrew on the way to practice. The truth was her knee felt just fine. The ice and rest had done the trick.

Val was dying to play. Gabriela had called again, and Miguel convinced Val to agree to go kick around in the gym after school tomorrow. Val could tell her father was really worried about her. He wasn't normally this involved. Initially, Val was resistant to playing with the El Fuego girls. She felt a little guilty even considering it. But Miguel reminded her that they were talking about starting a team at her school and would need her. Plus Val had to admit she liked Gabriela, and more than that she really liked being wanted. It felt better than how she was feeling about the Breakers. "Confused" was putting it mildly. She wondered if Makena had practiced her penalty kicks. She hoped Chloe was working on her defense. Those long ballerina legs had a tendency to stab at the ball. She tried not to think about Jessie and how happy she must have been that Val wasn't there.

Val pushed her math book aside and picked up her English novel, *The Good Earth* by Pearl S. Buck. It was a reading assignment about a family in China before World War II. She was almost done and hoped that Wang Lung and O-Lan would distract her. For the next few minutes she lost herself in ancient Chinese traditions, rubbing her toes occasionally as she read about how girls in China had their feet bound, tied up in bandages to keep them small and dainty. It sounded like torture. Ouch. No girl soccer playing in those days.

The kitchen door opened.

"I'm still fine, Papi!" Val said automatically. Her father had been checking on her constantly.

"It's me," a voice said, and Makena Walsh came into the kitchen, plopping her backpack on the table. "Man, this thing weighs a ton," she said with a sigh. "How's the knee?"

"Better," Val said. "It's pretty much all better."

"Oh, good, we are so totally going to need you this weekend. Lily found out who we are playing in the indoor championship, and you will not believe it!"

"Who?" Val asked.

"It's a team called the Showoffs."

"Oh, come on. Seriously?"

"Yep. Can you believe that?"

Val shook her head.

"And it's really just a winter select team made up from girls from…" Makena did a drumroll with her fingers on the table. Val held her breath. "…the Lions!"

"Nooo!" Val said. The Leewood Lions were the Breakers' archnemesis. During the outdoor season and at many tournaments, the two teams constantly battled for first place.

Makena nodded knowingly and said with a smile, "We need you, dude."

Val was so happy to see her friend. She couldn't wait to take on Leewood. She and Makena would make some magic up front, and on defense Jasmine and Jessie would be solid…

Jessie.

"And then we have the dance later that night," Makena went on. "I hope I don't scrape up my knee on the turf. I already have a good one from last week, and my mom keeps chasing me around with honey. It's, like, her new favorite thing."

Val's laugh was a little forced. She thought of the dance.

Makena, Chloe, and Jessie shopping. Val had forgotten it was all happening this weekend. Oblivious, Makena lifted up her leg to show Val the impressive turf burn on her right knee.

"Nice one," Val said. Then she noticed that Makena was wearing a bandanna around her ankle. She pointed to it and asked, "Torn sock?"

Makena smiled. "No, you couldn't be there today, so I wore a bandanna. Chloe did too. It looks cool. We're thinking of wearing them to the dance!"

Val sighed. Instead of being flattered by the bandanna, she was annoyed by the dance. "Is everyone still talking about this? Jeez. It feels like this dance is way more important than our team lately."

Makena nodded. "Yeah, I can't wait for it to be over. I'm so glad that I asked someone early. You should see how stressed out and obsessed everyone at school is. There are only a few more days. Jessie is the worst."

"She didn't find her secret date yet? She wouldn't even tell me who she wanted to ask," Val said. "Like I care."

"Oh, get this. Poor Chloe is stuck right in the middle. Jessie finally fessed up that she is, like, dying to ask Andrew. She was supposed to do it after practice tonight. When I left, she looked so nervous I thought she was going to throw up. She thinks he knows and is avoiding her."

"Andrew Gordon?" Val asked.

"Yeah, Andrew. Mr. Cool. Chloe's brother."

"Jessie is going to the dance with Andrew Gordon?" Val asked. Her voice was louder and more urgent. Suddenly she did care. A lot.

Makena answered, "I don't know. She said she was going to ask him today after practice. But Chloe thinks he likes someone else."

A wave of jealousy flooded Val, and she tried to hide her shock. Jessie and Andrew Gordon.

"Mac, there's something you should know," Val said. She took a deep breath. "Jessie is the real reason I didn't come to practice tonight."

Makena looked confused. "I thought you were hurt."

"No, I am," Val said. "I…was. But now I'm not. I'm fine."

"I don't get it," Makena said. "Didn't you tell Coach you hurt your knee again?"

"Yes. No. I don't know. I *can* play. My dad wanted me to rest." Val said. She didn't want Makena to worry about the championship. "See, look, I'm fine. I'm going to play tomorrow after school with El Fuego. I just needed a break today."

"El Fuego? What? What are you talking about, Val?"

Makena asked, her voice getting louder. "We have the biggest game of the indoor season coming up, and you skipped practice tonight and instead are going to play with a different team tomorrow? Because of Jessie? This makes no sense."

Val shook her head. "I've been trying to talk to you about this, Mac. It's bad. Jessie has been super harsh to me lately."

"About what?" Makena asked. "She's been weird to everyone lately. She's sucking up to Chloe to get to Andrew, which, of course, totally backfired. She's just totally out of control about this dumb dance. We're all sick of it."

Val could tell Makena wasn't getting it. "But, Mac, it's not about the dance. After the last game, she said that I didn't belong on the Breakers anymore. She said because I live in a different town and go to a different school I shouldn't be on the team."

Makena frowned.

"She said you and Chloe believe that too but that you just don't want to hurt my feelings."

Val waited for Makena to say something. She was staring at Val, mouth open. The two girls stared at one another for what felt like forever. "Well," Makena said at last. "That is the dumbest thing I have ever heard in my life."

Val was surprised to hear anger in her voice. Makena had more to say. "How could you believe *that*? Val, you are my best friend in the whole world. You always have been."

"I know," Val said.

"Do you really need me to tell you that? How could you believe I don't want you on the team? This is crazy." She was talking with her hands now and pacing around the small office.

"Well, you went to the mall with Jessie and Chloe!"

"So what!" Makena yelled. "What does that have to do with anything?"

"You didn't tell me," Val said, and something about Makena's demeanor changed. She looked at the ground. She fiddled with her fingers. "Why didn't you tell me?" Val asked again.

"Well, I…" Makena stammered. "We just went right before the game on Saturday. It's not a big deal. I still don't see what this has to do with the Breakers."

"Hold on a second. You went on Saturday? Saturday morning?"

Makena bit her lip.

Tears welled up in Val's eyes. She knew there had been more to this. She got it now. Saturday morning had been the Man U/Man City match. Makena had said she couldn't come watch because she had to do her chores. She had lied to Val.

Val looked at her friend. Makena looked back down at the floor.

"Val," she said finally. "I'm sorry. I just—"

"Just what?" Val asked in a small voice.

"I don't know. I guess I didn't want to make it worse that you weren't going to the dance. It sucks that we can't go to the same school."

"So you lied to me?" Val asked, crushed.

"Look, I'm sorry," Makena said. "I didn't want to hurt your feelings…"

There they were. Those three terrible words again. Val snapped.

"Let me get this straight. You lied to me about shopping because you didn't want to hurt my feelings? So I'm supposed to believe that part but not that you don't want me on the team. Maybe you don't want to hurt my feelings about that either. Don't you get it, Makena? That's exactly what Jessie said. Why can't you understand? I don't know who to trust anymore!"

"But what Jessie said isn't true!" Makena shouted.

"Well, guess what. You don't get to decide what I believe!" Val shouted in return, her own anger boiling over.

She got up to leave. "You lied to me! I cannot believe you of all people would do that!" Val gathered up her books and shoved them into her bag.

"Val, don't go!"

Val paused at the door and looked sadly back at her friend. "You know," she said, "maybe Jessie is right. Maybe I don't belong anymore."

11

Val hesitated before entering the gym. She could hear kids laughing and the slaps of balls on the hard floor and was a little confused when it sounded a lot more like basketball than soccer. Bending down, she checked her laces and shin guards one more time and straightened out her shirt.

"What am I supposed to even wear?" she had asked her father that morning before school.

Her dad was busy in the kitchen and just shrugged. "Who cares what you wear?"

"Papi, what if they are all wearing the same thing and I am the only one wearing a different color?"

Miguel had been hurriedly packing her lunch and getting himself ready for work. He looked up.

"*M'ija…*" he started. But seeing the worried look on

Val's face, his tone softened. "Oh. You should definitely wear your Mexico jersey. Or your Barca one."

"No way. That would make me look like I was trying too hard," Val said, rushing back into her room and frantically opening and closing her dresser drawers but finding nothing.

"Oh, right. Of course," Miguel said with a shake of his head. "Trying too hard."

In the end, Val had settled on a red T-shirt from a soccer camp she'd attended the previous summer. She figured any team named El Fuego was going to be red like fire. She tucked in her shirt now as she peered through the glass of the gym door to see the girls inside wearing shirts of all different colors and felt a little silly for worrying.

She took a deep breath. *This is it*, she thought. *Here we go.*

Val pulled at the door.

It didn't budge.

She hesitated. *Maybe the door being locked is a sign*, she thought. *This is a mistake. I should go home.* An image of Makena flashed in her mind. She would definitely tell me to turn around.

"It's just a kick-around," Val muttered to herself, giving the door another yank.

She felt it budge. It wasn't locked, just stuck. She gave it another tug and then thought again about Makena. So what if she's mad? She doesn't own me. She's the one who lied to me. About shopping and who knows what else.

Val wrenched the door open.

It worked, but the force of the pull sent Val flying backward, and her water bottle careened out of her bag, onto her foot, and went skidding into the gym.

The bouncing balls stopped.

"Uh, hey, Valentina," Gabriela said with a laugh as she and the rest of the girls looked amused at Val's big entrance. Gabriela scooped up the water bottle, took a fake swig, and said, "Thanks! I needed that."

Val tried to play it off with a joke. "Yeah, you looked thirsty."

The rest of the girls went back to playing basketball, and Gabriela jogged over and handed her the bottle, "Here you go. I'm glad you could make it today."

"Yeah, me too," Val answered sincerely. "I take any chance to play, especially in the winter."

"Cool," Gabriela answered. "Come over and meet everyone. A few people are still showing up."

Gabriela led her over to the group. "This is Denise, Alicia, Marta, Elizabeth, and Veronica." Val waved. She recognized the girls from their game. Denise was an awe-some goalie, and Marta was their tough center defender.

"Let's play HORSE," Alicia said. "You want to play?"

"Sure…" Val started to answer.

"Guys," Gabriela put her hands up, "Coach said no basketball, remember?"

"He's not here," Marta pointed out, turning to try a layup.

"Turn on the music!" Elizabeth yelled.

Gabriela shrugged and ran over to a small set of speak-ers attached to a phone. She fiddled with the phone for a few minutes, and the latest Justin Bieber hit started blaring.

The girls were suddenly dancing and shooting baskets, and while she wasn't exactly sure what she was supposed to do, Val found herself singing along and throwing her ball up toward the net.

A few minutes later the gym door opened and their coach, Juan, walked in. Without missing a beat, all the girls put the ball on their feet and started juggling.

So much for basketball. Val wondered if he would also make them turn off the music.

Instead, Juan came over to Val and motioned for her to pass the ball.

"Great to see you here," he said as the ball rolled up

his foot and he began to juggle the ball between his thighs. Then he passed it back to Val and called the team over.

"Sorry I was late," he said. "So much traffic around here. Everyone, I'm sure you remember or know Valentina." Val was amused that they were calling her Valentina. Only her grandmother usually did that.

"Let's start with a game of *Último*," he said.

¿Último? Val knew that meant "last or last one" in Spanish.

"We'll just play in this half of the gym." He looked at Val. "This is how we play. You just have to dribble your ball around, and don't let anyone take it from you. At the same time, try to kick everyone else's ball out of bounds, which in this case is to the other side of the court. The last one with the ball wins. Got it?"

Val nodded. She'd played a version of this before and was usually really good at controlling the ball.

"OK, remember, girls, you have to be able to keep your eyes up and not just on the ball to see what's happening around you. If you just look down, you can't see an opponent coming. OK, play!"

Val dribbled the ball using the inside and outside of both feet to keep it moving. She didn't try and steal anyone else's ball at first, wanting to get a feel for playing on the slick gym floor. It didn't take long for the other players to come after her. First Elizabeth dribbled close and then lunged for Val's ball. Val moved deftly to the side, but Alicia was waiting and swiftly kicked Val's ball out of bounds. She was the first one knocked out!

Val moved to the sidelines to watch the rest of the battle. Elizabeth was on attack, but she left her ball too open and Gabriela swooped in and sent it out of bounds. Val was impressed by the technical skills of the girls. They had great ball control. As good or maybe even better than the Breakers players did.

Denise won the first round, and Juan called the girls in. They were all laughing and breathing heavily after the first warm-up round.

"Did you see what worked and what didn't in there?" he asked. "Let's try another round."

The girls all nodded, and Val silently vowed to keep her eyes up as much as possible. She didn't want to get knocked out again.

Juan blew the whistle, and Val moved faster this time, keeping her eyes on the ball but frequently glancing up to see who was coming.

Gabriela came first, but Val was able to protect the ball with her body.

"Nice shielding, Val," Juan said.

Denise was next, but again, Val was able to keep herself between the ball and her attacker. She kept moving.

She noticed that Elizabeth was off her ball, trying to corner Alicia, and instead of being defensive, Val decided to attack. She dribbled over and quickly kicked Elizabeth's ball to the other side of the gym.

"Oh, man," Elizabeth said. "I'm out."

In just a few minutes, just Val and Gabriela were left. The music was still playing, and all the girls on the sidelines were cheering.

"¡*Vamos*, Val!" one of them shouted. Val didn't dare take her eyes off the ball or Gabriela.

"¡*Dale!*" Juan encouraged Val and Gabriela to engage.

Gabriela lunged for Val's ball, and Val moved quickly to the side. But the ball got away from her, and Gabriela moved in. Val got there first and got the ball back on her feet.

The cheers got louder. Val was breathing hard now.

"Let's go, Gabriela!" someone yelled.

Val felt Gabriela approach from the side and give her a good shoulder-to-shoulder shove. Val held her ground and then heard Gabriela laugh.

"I'm so tired," she whispered.

Val answered, "Me too."

Val was exhausted. It was one of the most strenuous drills she'd ever played.

Gabriela said, "Let's both win."

"OK, on three," Val said, slowing her pace and putting her foot on top of the ball to stop it.

Together the girls counted.

One. Two. Three.

Val ran toward Gabriela's ball, and Gabriela ran toward Val's ball. They looked at each other and nodded.

"Go!"

At exactly the same time they both kicked the ball, sending them out of bounds. They turned to look at one another and then yelled, "*¡Últimas!*"

Juan laughed and went over to turn off the music.

"*Muy bien*," he said. "Are we warmed up now?"

The rest of practice was just as fun. They played several fun games, and before long, Val found herself forgetting she was just there for a kick-around. Her love of the game erased her previous doubts, and she had to admit, she felt really comfortable and happy with the girls from El Fuego. She enjoyed the mix of English and Spanish the girls used at practice and just how nice they all were. She thought it was funny they called her Valentina sometimes.

As she gathered her belongings after practice, Juan approached.

"You are welcome to come anytime," he said. "I hope you had fun."

Val answered, "I had a great time, actually."

"You're a great player with really strong technical skills. You fit right in."

"Thanks," Val said. After the past few weeks, it was great to feel so happy about soccer and friends again.

Val started to move toward the exit when Juan stopped her.

"Val, you know you would always have a place on the El Fuego team if you wanted one."

Val didn't know what to say. She was startled. She felt like she should scream, "I'm a Breaker! I'm a Soccer Sister!" But something kept her quiet. Instead she just nodded.

"Think about it," Juan said.

"OK," Val answered truthfully. "I will."

12

Game time was at 11:00 a.m. the next Saturday. Val turned on the television hoping to be distracted by Zarco and Manchester United. She watched the last few minutes of the game. Manchester United was up by three goals, so Zarco was on the bench. Sleet was falling. He looked cold. She wondered if he ever felt like the odd man out living in dreary, wet England. They probably didn't even have any good hot dogs.

"*Vámonos, m'ija*," Miguel called from the hallway. They were headed to breakfast. It was almost ten.

Val was in limbo. She'd talked it over with her coach and her father and explained to Coach Lily she wasn't sure she was going to play in the game today. Miguel filled her in on what had been going on with Jessie. Lily said she was going to have a talk with Jessie and hoped Val would change her mind and come to the game. Val knew her father also wanted her to play and knew Mac had called a few times.

Val walked slowly to the car. Her knee felt fine, but her insides felt tortured and twisted. She'd never been so confused. She waited for her father to unlock the door. The outside of the car was caked with winter mud. She wrote "Breakers" on the door with her index finger.

"Papi, why don't you get a new car?" Val asked. "We can't afford it?"

Miguel smirked as he got behind the wheel. "I love this car," he said. "I will never give up this car."

Val sighed. "It's a piece of junk."

Miguel started the engine, his smile spreading. He backed up, looking in the rearview mirror to make sure traffic was clear. "To you it is junk," he said. "To me it is *un tesoro*. A treasure!"

Val shook her head in disgust. She was pensive and quiet during the drive to breakfast. Images from her afternoon with El Fuego flashed in her mind.

"*Ya llegamos*," Miguel said as he pulled into the parking lot of a small diner, their usual breakfast spot. "Let me tell you about my piece of junk," Miguel said as they walked inside. "When I came to this country, I had nothing. Only you, my precocious daughter. I didn't have many skills. I didn't speak much English. I had to find a way to take care of you and to survive. I worked in the restaurants because they would hire me. But I had a plan. I watched. I studied how to be a great chef. It wasn't easy, but I was determined to succeed. I had no choice."

The host showed them to their favorite booth. The waiter arrived with coffee for Miguel, juice for Val, and a smile for his favorite customers. His name was Johnny, and he knew no menus were required.

"The regular?" he asked. Miguel and Val nodded. Miguel always got the vegetarian omelet with a side of ham, and Val, the blueberry pancakes with a dollop of whipped cream.

The waiter poured coffee for Miguel while the pit in her stomach grew. She watched as the steam from her father's mug swirled and twisted in the space and silence between them. Val didn't look up but could feel his eyes on her. She watched as he took a small sip.

"*¡Y lo logre!* I did it," Miguel said suddenly.

"Did what?" Val asked, startled. He smiled and continued in Spanish, "When I became the manager at Rosa's, many years ago, I finally had enough money to buy a car. No longer did I have to take the bus or walk in the cold winter." Miguel took another sip and kept talking. "I went with the money my hard work had earned me, and I bought this car. It was used. It wasn't perfect. But it was mine. I had earned it. I love it for what it stands for, *m'ija*, not for what it looks like."

The food arrived quickly. Val picked up her fork but then put it down again. "I'm sorry, Papi, for making fun of your car. I never knew that."

"Do not be sorry," Miguel said, wiping his chin. "It is a terrible car. But sometimes, you just have to change the way you see something. When you see my car, you are embarrassed. When I drive my car, I am proud. You understand?"

Val nodded. She did understand now. Val thought again about Gabriela. She couldn't help but notice that they had the same exact hair color. The same color eyes. The same warm-brown skin. El Fuego was a team full of joy and friendship, just like the Breakers. She felt at home with El Fuego, like she belonged.

Miguel got up to pay the check. Val fiddled with the straw in her orange juice. She knew her father was happy she had gone to play with El Fuego. To miss the Breakers' championship game would make quite a statement, even if it was during the optional indoor season. Val didn't doubt her love for the Breakers or Makena and the rest of the team except Jessie. Yet she had come to realize none of the drama would have gotten to her if she hadn't already had some serious doubts of her own.

Maybe it wouldn't be so bad to play in her own town, and El Fuego was good, and the players were nice. Wouldn't that be a good team too? Couldn't they be her Soccer Sisters?

Her father returned, and together they walked outside. Val knew the moment was coming. The teams were arriving and would be warming up soon. She walked over to the clunker. The car she had been so embarrassed by. It was still old. It was still dirty. It really was still a piece of junk. But she could see why he had always loved it. She loved it too now. She walked around to the back.

"We can never sell it," Val said with a smile. Then she made a face and added, "But we can wash it."

Miguel nodded with a grin. "There is one more special thing about my car I want to show you." Miguel pointed to the trunk. "It's in there."

"Open it!" Val said, trying not to look at her watch, knowing it must be close to game time.

Miguel pressed the button to open the trunk. At first Val didn't see anything special, but then she did. Her Breakers soccer bag! The blue-and-yellow one with the awesome Soccer Sisters tag. She looked at her father. "Now, *you* open it," he said. Val obeyed. She felt the familiar joy of looking inside. There was her Breakers uniform. Her indoor shoes. Her shin guards. Her ball. A brand-new bottle of water and, of course, clean, beautiful new socks.

Val sighed and asked her dad, "You think I should play today?"

"That is totally up to you. But I have never seen a longer or sadder face on my child. I think you should listen to Makena, not to that other girl, and I think you should listen to your heart."

He was right. Val had known it the minute she saw her bag. While she was excited to get to know the El Fuego girls better and hoped they started a school team, in her heart Val was a Breaker.

She smiled at her father. "*Gracias*, Papi," she said.

They got in the car. Miguel turned to his daughter. He was beaming and had a funny look on his face, a sort of know-it-all half grin.

"Why are you looking at me like that?" Val asked.

Miguel shook his head and raised his shoulders. "Oh, no reason. I just love you, *m'ija*."

13

Val slipped into Total Sport unnoticed. She headed toward the locker room to get changed. She could see the Showoffs and the Breakers warming up on the far field. The sidelines were packed with spectators. She saw her father heading over to the field and wondered if Mac or any of the Breakers had spied him. She slipped on her jersey, relishing the coolness of her number as it slid down her back. Her protective soccer shield back in place. She sat on the bench and laced up her shoes, going through her special pregame ritual. She could hear Makena's voice in her head, urging her to hurry up already.

Val took a deep breath. She was ready. Ready to face Jessie and ready to face the truth. And the truth was that Jessie had been acting like a bully. Her lies hurt so much because they had hit too close to home. Val did often feel left out, she did feel vulnerable and different, and she knew now that this was an insecurity she would have to accept and overcome. Val checked her headband in the mirror, put her street clothes in her bag, and took another deep breath.

"Game on," she said to herself.

She slung her bag on her back, grabbed her ball, and headed toward the field. Mac was the first to see her. She grabbed Chloe by the shirt and pointed. Chloe smiled and poked Jasmine. One by one the Breakers looked Val's way. Lily beamed as Val approached. As she got closer, she saw Makena hold up her fingers and heard her count, "One! Two! Three!" All the girls on the field screamed in unison, "Val!"

Makena ran over to hug Val. Val held her friend tightly, and at exactly the same time, they both whispered, "I'm sorry."

Makena hugged Val back and said, "No sorries. You're here. That's what matters. I'm lost without you, Val. I should have told you about my dress and everything. I should have known you would have just been excited for me."

Val nodded and then spied Jessie on the bench.

Makena turned to look. "I'm pretty sure she's benched.

When she got here today, Lily gave her a really long and special 'think time.'"

"Oh, brother, now she's going to hate me more," Val said.

"No, she won't." Makena said. "She's got her own problems. Don't let her get to you anymore."

"I won't," Val said firmly. Chloe ran over to join them.

"Check this out," she said, lifting her leg all the way up to her head.

"You are freakishly flexible, Chloe," Makena said. "Like, it hurts me to see you do that."

"Ballerina!" Chloe replied with a giggle and then pointed to her ankle. "We've all got them on. Here's yours."

Chloe handed Val a blue-and-yellow bandanna that matched their uniform colors. "We got one for everyone and made Jessie wear one too. Ha!"

Val looked at all her teammates and beamed. Each one had a bandanna on her ankle. Any lingering doubts evaporated.

"Is the ref going to let us wear them?" Val asked. Just then the whistle blew.

"We'll find out," Chloe said excitedly. "Let's go!"

The Breakers took the field. Val and Chloe were up front. Makena took her spot in the midfield. Jasmine and Harper were on defense, and Ariana was in the goal. Jessie was looking glum on the bench.

Val sized up the Showoffs. Sure enough, a girl named Lindsey, the Leewood superstar, was starting with the ball.

"Oh, this is going to be fun," Val said to herself. She made eye contact with Makena. Makena nodded. *La abeja* was ready to sting.

The referee blew the whistle to start the game, and from the first seconds the Breakers were on fire. They were attacking from all angles and making incredible passes, and they had so many chances to score. But by halftime, the score was still 0 to 0. They couldn't get the ball in the net. During the brief halftime, the girls had only a few minutes to grab a sip of water and switch sides. Val grabbed her water bottle and took a long, satisfying gulp.

"Why'd you even come back?" a voice asked. She knew it was Jessie.

Val finished her sip, took a deep breath, and said, "I never left. This is my team, Jessie. I'm a Breaker."

Val felt a presence come up behind her. Makena Walsh. Val looked over her shoulder and went on, "If you can't be a Soccer Sister, then *you* should leave. You don't have to like me. But I belong here, and nothing you say will ever change that."

Makena put her arm around Val.

"It's team first, Jessie," Makena said. "If you don't get that, then Val's right. You're the one who doesn't belong."

Val and Makena walked together back onto the field. Makena looked behind her. "We'll see about her," Makena said. "We wanted Lily to kick her off the team, but she said Jessie deserves another chance."

"I doubt she's going to change. I just hope I can play with her again. I honestly don't know," Val said.

"Just remember Code number seven."

Val nodded. "Right. Leave it on the field."

"Yeah, just play. Forget everything else."

The second-half whistle blew, and the Breakers were back in action. It took a few minutes for Val to shake off what had happened at halftime. She knew Jessie was right about one thing. Val *was* different. But different was great. She was proud of herself, her family, and where she came from and would never doubt her place on the Breakers or anywhere else again.

"Val! I'm open!" Chloe called from the outside. She was making a smart run up the flank. Val fed the ball through two defenders, and Chloe went for the corner and then crossed the ball with her left foot, and Makena nearly got a head on it. They were getting closer.

The Showoffs got a goal kick because the Breakers'

ball went out of bounds over the goal line. Molly Barrelton took the kick, and it went all the way over the midfield line. *That girl has a big foot*, Val thought. The Showoffs' forward gathered the ball, and Harper tried to chase her down. She went in for a tackle and missed. The ball went out of bounds, but Harper stayed down.

The referee called their coach onto the field, and Lily rushed to Harper's side. All the Breakers took a knee and then clapped when Harper was able to stand.

"I think she sprained her ankle," Chloe said, walking over to Val. They watched as Lily accompanied Harper to the sidelines. Their coach said something to Jessie, who jumped up from the bench.

"Oh, great," Val muttered. Jessie was coming in. *Leave it on the field*, Val said to herself. *Leave it on the field. Just play the game.*

"¡*Vamos*, Breakers!" Miguel yelled from the sidelines. Val smiled at her father. Then she noticed that Andrew Gordon was standing next to him. He grinned at her. She started to smile back, but then she remembered Jessie and the dance. She looked away. Jessie was taking her place on the field.

He's probably here to watch her, Val realized. *Forget that.*

Jasmine threw the ball down the line, and Jessie made a good first touch. She had always been a good dribbler,

Val had to admit. She tracked Jessie down the line, calling, "Cross!"

Jessie looked up, saw it was Val, and didn't make the pass. She kept dribbling and finally lost the ball.

Lily yelled from the sidelines, "Don't hold on to it for so long, Jessie!"

As the game went on, Jessie's selfish play continued. She wouldn't pass. She kept moving too far forward and getting caught offside. Makena's and Val's eyes met. Makena shook her head in disgust. It was obvious Jessie was refusing to pass to Val, and the Breakers needed a goal. Time was running out. They had come so close so many times but weren't getting their shots off. They were a passing team, and with just one player being selfish, the entire squad was thrown off.

"Breakers, we have got to pass the ball!" Makena called to her teammates, although she was really directing her message to Jessie. The Showoffs were starting to sense that the Breakers were out of sync. They were experienced enough to know that an arguing team is a vulnerable team.

Molly Barrelton was one of the best players in the league. She got the ball about twenty yards out and let loose a screamer. Val watched as it headed toward the goal. There was no spin on the ball, and that meant that Molly had hit it perfectly. The ball headed straight to the upper-right corner. Ariana dove to her left, her arms outstretched, her feet off the ground. But she couldn't reach the ball. Val held her breath as the ball arrived. Because of the lack of spin, it flew just an inch too high and clanged against the cross bar with a terrible crash. The goalposts shook, the crowd gasped, and the rebound flew long. The ball bounced back all the way out to midfield.

Jessie was there. She gathered the ball and looked up to make a pass.

"Send me, Jessie!" Val called. She could see Jessie's mind working. Val knew the last thing Jessie wanted to do was give Val the ball. Luckily her soccer instincts finally overrode her pettiness, and she sent a beautiful through ball to Val. Val pounced and headed downfield. She knew the time was now.

The Breakers moved forward as a team, and Val could hear the spectators going crazy on the sidelines. She beat the two midfielders and then slowed down when she got about twenty yards out. The defenders were trying to slow her down. Val kept control of the ball, pulling it back and looking for a pass.

"Square!" she heard a voice call. She looked up and saw Jessie was making a perfect run from the back. She wanted Val to put the ball at her feet, across the face of the goal. With no hesitation, Val made her pass and timed it perfectly. Without breaking stride, Jessie was able to take a first-time shot. She hit it with her right foot. Well. The ball stayed low and hard, and the Showoff goalie had no chance.

The Breakers finally got their goal!

Jessie jumped high in the air, her arms overhead in celebration. All the Breakers came to hug her. The crowd screamed and whistled in appreciation. Val hung back, but she cheered and clapped with the rest of her team.

The final whistle blew, and the crowds flooded the fields. Miguel gave Val a tight hug and told her how proud he was of her. The Breakers had secured their first-ever indoor championship.

After the game, Jessie approached Val as she was picking up her ball.

"Nice pass," Jessie said.

"Nice shot," Val responded calmly.

Jessie nodded and walked away.

It wasn't great, Val thought, *but it was a start.*

Mac ran up behind Val and jumped on her back like a baby monkey trying to hold on to its mother. "That was awesome!" she yelled. "Oh, how I love beating that team."

Mac jumped down and then put her arm around Val.

Mac turned Val around, and she could feel she was being led somewhere.

"Where are we going?" Val asked, peering over her shoulder at Jessie.

"Just come with me a second, OK?" Mac answered, urging Val toward the exit.

Val's steps felt lighter as she walked with Mac, a feeling she hadn't had in a while. But then she looked over her shoulder again.

Jessie was grabbing her bag from the bench.

"Hang on a second. I need to go talk to Jessie," Val said.

Mac pulled her along, "I need to show you something."

Val stopped. "Give me a minute, OK?"

Their eyes met, and Mac nodded.

"Meet us… I mean, meet me by the front, OK?"

"Yeah, I'll be right there." Val jogged over to Jessie.

"Hey," Val said, "What a good game. That was a nice shot."

"Thanks. You gave me the perfect pass," Jessie answered.

"We make a good team sometimes," Val said.

Jessie didn't answer at first.

Val hesitated and looked at her cool neon indoor shoes. Unsure of what to say next, she turned to go.

Jessie said, "I'm sorry I told you no one wanted you on the team. It's not true, you know?"

"Yeah, I know."

"You're a really good player. Anyone would want to have you on her team."

"Thanks," Val answered sincerely.

"Well, I gotta go," Jessie said. "I'll see you around."

Jessie walked away. Val watched her go. I guess this was as good as it was going to get for now. *I guess I don't have to be best friends with everyone either.* Val smiled to herself. She had just thought of something else to add to the Soccer Sisters Code…

Val looked around for Mac and her father but didn't see anyone by the entrance.

"Hey, nice assist," someone said nearby. Andrew Gordon was standing in front of her.

"Thanks," she said. "How's my hero, Bubba, today?"

"He's a little beat-up, but he's tough," Andrew said in mock seriousness. Val noticed that he had a small cut over his eye.

"What happened?" Val asked.

"Someone hit me, and my helmet cut my face," Andrew said with a shrug. "No biggie."

Val looked closer. "You really should put some honey on that."

"Honey?" Andrew asked with a laugh.

"Yes, it has very good healing properties," Val said in her most professorial tone.

"Really?"

"Yes, really."

"Good to know," Andrew said. "Maybe I'll try it."

Andrew and Val stared at each other for a few seconds, and then Val started to unlace her cleats to change into her boots. No more slipping on the ice for her.

Andrew leaned on his stick. "So when you weren't at practice the other night, I was a little worried and came by Rosa's."

"You did?" Val asked, surprised. Neither Makena nor Miguel had said anything about that.

"I talked to Makena, and she told me you had just left."

"Huh" was Val's only baffled response.

"I guess you worked everything out with your team?"

"Yeah, we did."

"That's good," Andrew said. He started fiddling with his shoes. Val finally spied her father watching their conversation.

"Well, I guess I should get going," she said.

"Val?" Andrew said.

Val turned back around. "Please don't tell me I have sticks in my hair again."

"Nope," he said, smiling. "I wanted to ask you something. Or actually, I want *you* to ask *me* something."

Val heard rustling behind her. She turned to see Makena and Chloe and all the Breakers standing in a group, giggling. Makena nodded. She was holding something behind her back. Chloe was standing on her toes, clapping her hands together. The two of them looked like they were about to explode with giddiness. Slowly, Makena moved her arms to the front. She was holding a bag. Val watched as Makena unzipped the bag and showed her what was inside.

"We did a little more shopping!" Chloe and Makena screamed together.

Makena was holding up a hanger, and on it was the beautiful butterfly dress. The fabric shimmered, catching the overhead lights like stars on a perfect night. She found her father's eyes as tears began to fill her own.

He looked very pleased with himself. Val grinned and nodded. A feeling of warmth and gratitude filled her soul. She looked at her team. Her friends. Makena. Chloe. Oh, how she loved her Soccer Sisters, and she knew they loved her.

She turned back to Andrew and found him standing close. Directly in front of her. He was smiling, clearly in on it all. He smiled and said, "So what do you say, Man U girl? Wanna dance?"

Soccer Sisters Team Code

1. Team first.
2. Don't be a poor sport or loser.
3. Play with each other and don't take the fun out of it.
4. Never put someone down if they make a mistake.
5. Practice makes perfect.
6. Never give up on the field or on one another.
7. Leave it on the field.
8. Always do the right thing.
9. Bring snacks on assigned days.
10. Beat the boys at recess soccer.

Book Club Questions and Activities

1. Why do you think Makena lied to Val about going to the mall with Chloe and Jessie? Is it ever OK to lie in order to protect a friend's feelings?

2. In your opinion, would Val be betraying the Soccer Sisters Team Code if she were to join the team at her school? Why or why not?

3. What do you think is the best way for Val to handle her relationship with Jessie in the future?

4. What makes an object special or meaningful to someone, in the way that Val's father's car is important to him? What is an object that is special to you and why?

5. Why do you think it is so difficult for Val to talk to Makena about her problems with Jessie and about feeling excluded from the Soccer Sisters?

6. What do you think is the most important rule on the Soccer Sisters Team Code and why?

7. Why do you think a team doesn't play as well when its members aren't getting along?

8. Why do you think Jessie was so eager to exclude Val from the team?

9. Val criticizes "helicopter parents," parents who are too involved with their child's team. How involved do you think parents should be with their child's team?

10. Write your own sisterhood code with your team or group of friends!

The Sweet Science of Honey

Are any of you wondering which of Mrs. Walsh's wounds healed better: the one with the antibiotics or the one with the honey?

I may be a writer, but I really love science and nature. In fact, I was a biological anthropology major in college. Biological anthropology is the study of human beings and other animals and their behaviors. Some of the best classes I took were about social insects like ants and bees and how they work together. I mean talk about teamwork!

The reason I created Mrs. Walsh's character was so that I could share little nature tidbits with all of you.

So what do you think happened with her wound care? Well, I'm going to say that they probably both healed equally well. But, had she had only honey on one and nothing on the other, I would certainly say the one with the medicinal honey would have healed faster.

We are so lucky to have modern medicine, but it's also amazing to learn that there are natural remedies humans have been using for thousands of years—some of them thanks to bees!

Honey has been used since ancient times for wound care and to prevent infection dating back to before 2000 BC.

Even the famous Greek scientist and philosopher Aristotle wrote about honey, saying it was "good as a salve for sore eyes and wounds."

Eyes? That sounds sticky to me.

Manuka is the name of a special kind of honey that has even been reported to have antibacterial properties that fight infection. You can find it in some drug stores.

Check out this link if you want to learn more:

https://www.ncbi.nlm.nih.gov/pmc/articles
/PMC3609166/

Isn't that sweet?

Meet our Soccer Sisters Ambassador Brandi Chastain!

Brandi Chastain—NCAA, World Cup, and Olympic icon—is best known for her game-winning penalty kick against China in the 1999 FIFA Women's World Cup final. She also played on the teams that won the inaugural Women's World Cup in 1991, Olympic gold medals in 1996 and 2004, and the country's first professional women's league championship.

Chastain is currently the coach of the Bellarmine College Preparatory varsity boys' soccer team and was a color commentator on soccer telecasts for NBC and ABC/ESPN. In addition, Chastain is an active advocate for several causes that are important to her, including safe play and the education of concussion injuries, Crohn's disease and awareness of the illness especially in young children, and equal rights for women in sports.

Brandi is married to Jerry Smith, who is the women's soccer coach at her alma mater, Santa Clara University. She has one son, Jaden, and is also a volunteer assistant coach at Santa Clara.

Soccer Sisters Organization

Soccer Sisters aims to inspire and connect young girls and women through sports-based stories and experiences.

We are a for-profit social enterprise aimed at reaching sports-oriented young kids and women with inspiring products and experiences that give back. Our first set of products is the Soccer Sisters book series for middle grade children:

Out of Bounds
Caught Offside
One on One

To learn more about Soccer Sisters, please visit our website and our social handles:

soccersisters.com
Instagram @soccersisters.forever
facebook.com/soccersisters
Twitter @soccersisters

Part of being a Soccer Sister is giving back. Here are some great groups that are supporting soccer and girls all over the world. Check them out!

coachesacrosscontinents.org
Coaches Across Continents is a global leader in the sport for social impact movement.

goalsarmenia.org
Girls of Armenia Leadership Soccer (GOALS) empowers girls throughout the communities of Armenia, using soccer as a vehicle for change and opportunity.

oneworldplayproject.com
One World Play Project encourages the power of play all over the world.

ussoccerfoundation.org

The U.S. Soccer Foundation helps foster an active and healthy lifestyle, using soccer to cultivate critical life skills that pave the path to a better future.

fifa.com/womens-football/live-your-goals/index.html

FIFA inspires women and girls to play soccer and stay in the game.

goalsforgirls.org

Goals for Girls uses soccer to teach young women life skills on how to be agents of change in their own lives and in their communities.

Soccer Sisters Roster

BROOKVILLE BREAKERS

Makena Walsh

Valentina Flores

Chloe Gordon

Jessie Palise

Ariana Murray

Harper Jones

Sydney Lin

Abby Rosen

Tessa Jordan

Kat Emelin

Ella Devine

Jasmine Manikas

Coach Lily James

Glossary

50/50 ball: When a player from each team tries to win a loose ball (and they each have a 50/50 chance of doing so).

Assist: When a player gets the ball to a second player, who scores as a result of the pass.

Bench: Where the substitutes sit during the game.

Box: The box that is formed when a line is drawn eighteen yards out from each goalpost along the goal line. The lines extend eighteen yards into the field of play and are connected with a line that is parallel to the goal line.

Breakaway: When an offensive player is going to goal with the ball and has left all defenders behind. A rare and very exciting event!

Captain: The player or players who have been designated by the coach or team to lead and represent the team during a game. The captain is the only player allowed to speak to the referee. A captain is often given a distinctive arm band.

Caution: When the referee shows a yellow card to a player after a foul. It's a warning or "caution" to calm down and play by the rules. A player given two yellow cards in one game is ejected from the field! You don't want to get yellow cards.

Center circle: A circle with a ten-yard radius, drawn with the center mark as its center.

Clear: A term used by defenders to send the ball rapidly upfield. This term is yelled out by defenders to alert the defender with the ball that she has impending pressure.

Cleats: Shoes worn by soccer players. So called for the studs or cleats on the soles of the shoes that help grip the grass and prevent slipping.

Corner kick: A kick awarded to the attacking team when the ball, having last been touched by the defending team, crosses the goal line and goes out of bounds. The ball is placed in the corner, duh!

Cross: A ball that has been kicked or thrown (from a throw-in) from near the touch line toward the goal.

Crossbar: The structure of the goal that connects the two upright goalposts.

Dead ball situation: Any situation when the ball is put back into play. Sounds creepy but isn't.

Dive: When a player fakes being fouled and falls to the ground. Unfortunately, it happens all the time.

Dribble: Moving the ball forward with the feet (similar to basketball but with your feet!).

Far post: The goalpost that is farthest from the ball.

Forward: An offensive player playing closest to the opponent's goal.

Foul: An offense against an opponent or against the spirit of the game that results in a free kick.

Free kick: A method of restarting play.

Give-and-go: Just what it sounds like: A player passes to a teammate, runs, and gets the ball back from the same teammate. You "give" the ball, and then you "go."

Goal: 1. The structure defined by two up-right goalposts and one crossbar that is set on the goal line. 2. To score.

Goal kick: A kick awarded to the defensive team after the attacking team has put the ball over the defending team's goal line. Opposite of a corner kick, the ball is placed close to the goal. Duh number two.

Golden goal: The goal in "sudden victory" overtime that wins and ends the game.

Hand ball: When a player, not the goalie, touches the ball with a hand or part of the arm.

Header: Passing, clearing, controlling, or shooting the ball with the head. This has recently been outlawed for younger kids to prevent collisions and concussions.

Juggling: A practice skill when the ball is kept in the air using any legal part of the body.

Keep-away: A practice game where the object is for one side to retain possession rather than to score goals.

Near post: The goalpost that is nearest to the ball.

Nutmeg: When a player puts the ball through the legs of an opposing player, a player is said to have been "nutmegged" or "megged." Don't let this happen to you!

Offside: A player is called "offside" when she is nearer to her opponent's goal than both the ball and the second-last opponent. It's confusing for many parents and sometimes players and referees!

Own goal: A goal scored by a player into her own team's net. Very sad event.

Penalty kick: A shot is taken on goal as a result of a foul committed by the defensive team in its penalty area or "box." All players except the goalie and the player taking the kick must be outside the penalty area when the kick is taken. Penalty kicks are also called "PKs" or "penalties" and can be used to decide a tied championship game. They are very stressful yet exciting events.

Penalty mark: Also called the penalty spot. A circular mark nine inches in diameter made twelve yards out from the center of the goal where the ball is placed when a penalty kick is to be taken.

Red card: A red card is given to a player who has committed a serious foul or series of bad fouls during a game. A coach or even a parent can also get "red carded" for yelling at the referee or other bad behavior. Anyone who receives a red card must immediately leave the field. If a player receives a red card, her team must continue the game down a player, and she cannot play in the next game.

Shin guards: Protective equipment worn by players to aid in prevention of injuries to the shin.

Shot: An attempt to score on the opponent's goal.

Striker: A position name given to a player in a central attacking position.

Throw-in: When the ball is thrown in by the team that did not kick it out of bounds.

Yellow card: A cautionary measure used by the referee to warn a player not to repeat an offense. A second yellow card in a match results in a red card.

Acknowledgments

Thanks so much for reading *Caught Offside*! I hope you enjoyed Val's story and getting to know more of the team. By now, you have probably also figured out that nothing gets done without teamwork, and this series is no exception.

There are always so many people to thank, but I'll start with the biggies: the entire Sourcebooks team. Annie Berger, thank you for all your wonderful support and making the books so much better. Congrats on your own new team, and I wish you many years of happiness! Steve Geck, Sarah Kasman, Alex Yeadon, Katy Lynch, Beth Oleniczak, Elizabeth Boyer, Nicole Hower, and everyone at Jabberwocky who have made this series so special. Shane White, thanks for all your great ideas about bringing this book to so many clubs, camps, and leagues. Dominique Raccah, I'm proud to be part of a house that supports so many women writers.

My agent at Aevitas Creative, Lauren Sharp, thank you for always being my biggest supporter, and Ed Klaris at Klaris IP for all your incredible guidance.

Thanks to Lucy Truman for the fantastic cover art that really brings the fun and the girls to life.

Brandi Chastain, Stacey Vollman Warwick, Marian Smith, and Dan Love, thank you for your support of every part of Soccer Sisters. Brandi, you remain the ultimate role model for me and so many others. Stacey, your guidance and friendship mean so much to me. Marian, thank you for editing with humor and grace. I am so lucky to call you my sister. Dan Love, you are a true Soccer Sister! You have made a huge impact on my team, and I can't thank you enough. Chrystian Von Schoettler, your site development and logos are wonderful and you are a joy to work with.

As always, I would never be able to write these books without the support of my incredible husband, Diron, and our two kids, Lily and William. I am also very grateful to our large and loving extended family and their unending belief in the series and in me. Verenice Merino, you always inspire us with your love, smarts, and warmth, and you make our lives better every day. Paula Fernades, thank you for making everything so easy.

I believe that every kid—boy or girl—should have the

opportunity to play sports if they want to. The Girls of Armenia Leadership Soccer (GOALS) continues to fight for girls to have equal opportunities in the villages of Armenia. I am grateful for everyone who supports their dreams.

Coaches Across Continents, you are changing the lives of Soccer Sisters all over the world, and it's an honor to call myself a member of your team. Nick Gates, Nora Dooley, Kevin O'Donovan, Adam Burgess, Brian Suskiewicz, Markus, Judith and Bill Gates, and every single person at CAC, thank you for all you do to make the world a better place through sport.

I've also had the great support of many coaches and clubs here at home. Matt Popoli, Jon Feinstein, and everyone at NY Surf, thank you for supporting the books and sharing them with your players. Don Cupertino and everyone at Quickstrike FC, I'm grateful for your support with the Play It Forward Project and for believing in Soccer Sisters. Berkshire Soccer Academy for Girls, Positive Tracks, Soccer Without Borders, Syncitup Soccer, Soccer Girl Probs, the U.S. Soccer Foundation, Grassroots Soccer, Goals for Girls, and so many other fantastic organizations are making soccer a powerful vehicle for change around the world. Thank you for all you do to support girls and sports.

Don't miss the next book in
this great new series:

One on One

About the Author

Andrea Montalbano is a writer, advocate, coach, and soccer player. She grew up playing soccer in Miami and took that love to Harvard, where she was a cocaptain and a Hall of Famer. She then attended Columbia University's Graduate School of Journalism, kicking off a long career at NBC News as a writer, producer, and supervising producer for NBC News's *TODAY* program. Andrea left broadcast journalism to write books and authored *Breakaway* in 2010. Determined to create a series for girls, she spent the next few years writing the three Soccer Sisters novels. Off the field, Andrea is an activist for using sports for social change and has represented the U.S. government abroad to teach the importance of sports for girls. She is a founder of the Girls of Armenia Leadership Soccer charity and is also on several boards for Coaches Across Continents, a global leader in education through sports. She has enjoyed coaching her own two children on local club teams and lives with them and her husband, Diron Jebejian, outside New York City.